Arias, Arturo
After the bombs.

AFTER THE BOMBS

a novel by
ARTURO ARIAS

translated by Asa Zatz

CURBSTONE PRESS

The Spanish edition, *Después de las bombas*,
was published in 1979 by Editorial Joaquín Mortiz,
S.A., Mexico.

1995

translation © 1990 by Asa Zatz
ALL RIGHTS RESERVED
printed in the U.S. by BookCrafters

cover image: detail from a woodcut print by Naúl Ojeda

This publication was supported in part by donations, and
by grants from The National Endowment for the Arts and
the Connecticut Commission on the Arts, a state agency
whose funds are recommended by the Governor and
appropriated by the State Legislature.

91-B4783

ISBN: 0-915306-88-3 (cloth)
ISBN: 0-915306-89-1 (paper)
Library of Congress number 90-81428

Distributed to the trade by
The Talman Co.,
150 Fifth Ave., New York, NY 10011

Published by
Curbstone Press, 321 Jackson St., Willimantic, CT 06226

AFTER THE BOMBS

CHAPTER 1

1954

Carriage.

Infant.

Hives.

Never one alone. All three together. Always the three together prompting the screaming. Desperation. Passing him back and forth, he and she, taking him, giving him back, desperation, passing the screaming back and forth, back and forth endlessly, every morning, rain or shine, the screaming that those words provoked.

Carriage.

Infant.

Hives.

The little wicker carriage with netting over it. Every morning rain or shine. Shooing them off, the insects inevitably attracted, the sweetish odor of the bleeding scabs. Hives. And she. Her baby. Getting the same refrain from everyone. If you don't take care you're going to lose him, if you don't take care, you're going to lose him. As if we don't, as if we don't, because, always, all the never-ending time, rain or shine. The daily camomile bath. The scream of awakening. To bring down the swelling. And starting the exchange back and forth, scream upon scream upon scream. From one to the other, he and she. Dusting him with the special Swiss powder. Passing the baby back and forth, he to her to him. Swathing him in the finest gauze obtainable. And passing him back and forth again, always always. Teaspoonfuls of syrup. Screaming. Salves. And screaming. Pill. And screams and screams and screams.

And the husband. Putting on a brave front between one feeding bottle and the next. Waiting for breakfast, reading the morning paper, and little smile little smile that didn't hide the sadness, little smile little smile. Refried beans. Nothing wrong, nothing, absolutely nothing, a few little pustules, the baby in the carriage.

So long old girl. See you tonight.

Saying goodbye to him with a kiss. A wait. Resignation. Watching him trot off with his little bird steps, disappearing around the corner store on his cinnamon-stick legs. And now to set out on her long senseless walks. The man bound for the Palace. The route to the National Palace. And she watching him till he was gone. The mornings advancing, rain or shine. Hurrying, now. Wrapping baby in his little coverlets, her first-born, her darling, parrot-green little blankets, my little parrot, and into the carriage, faithful retainer of three generations. Three Sánchezes, including her husband with his big handlebar mustache and potbelly belly that grew and kept growing. Not a thinker, no. He worked. Fervent comrades building a dream that was blooming, hives notwithstanding, something to open one's eyes, her young office worker.

And hustling out to the street, gray, dirty street, arguments and hubbub, up and down, crossing every blessed alley, the hellish city. Along the avenues on even days. Along the streets on the odd. And that's the way she did it. Little step by step. Visiting, little step by step, all the doctors, desperately seeking the necessary medication nowhere to be found. The allergy would not go away. And looking for the next little shingle on a doorway God knows where. No luck there, either. Nothing. And she kept on, kept sweating, and the baby kept on, his little rag arms tied down to the carriage, wrists black and blue from pulling, pushing, pulling, pushing. But untied meant scratch, scratch until they bled. Protecting him even from himself. And her unusually long hair, so admired in better days, already beginning to look neglected and with a gray strand here and there. And she not even thirty. And friends in the street. That street, so public, so open. How's the baby doing? Unaware of the misty eyes, oblivious to the choked-up throat trying to spit out the slippery expressions of anguish, of unrelenting suffering. Let me have a look at him. And the pushing back of the hood, the expression of mute horror, the biting of the tongue to keep back the gagging, those pus-covered sores. And the comments, what a cute rattle or, such a pretty color that little coverlet or, what fine hair he has. And, have you been to see Dr. Lara yet? Yes. Very good, isn't he? Yes. My husband thinks he's the best children's doctor. Yes. They went to school

9

together as kids, can you imagine that? Yes. Of
course, if you've already been to him... Yes. Well, so
nice to see you. Yes. Yes. Yes. Now, moving on
quickly, to get lost in the crowd, little steps
resounding on the dirty pavement, one after another
after another, after another after another, and that's
how the seasons went by, pushing the little carriage
along the broad avenues and narrow alleys, pushing
the little carriage bippity-bop along the Avenue of
Desire bibbity-bop towards the Street of Bitterness,
bippity-bop past the Carmelite church, never
stopping, never giving up, never arriving at her
destination. Bippity-bop, the baby constantly fighting
for a cool breath from the thin air, his chest rising
and falling, rising and falling, eyes glazed, mouth
like pumice. And she went bippity-bop, ignoring the
winter rains and the hoots of derision, never held
back by student demonstrations, workers' protest
marches. She accepted her martyrdom stoically,
without bravado, without display, frozen into the
silence of a dream.

June. She was walking along the street the day
the Thunderbolts began bombarding the city.
Climbing the Street of Sighs with the tired little
carriage, Dr. Godoy that day, when she saw the little
silver dots gleaming among the clouds for the first
time. How pretty! Actually they did shine gloriously,
like the finest angel dust, that blue-white afternoon,
silently swinging in the north wind. And she, her
anxious eyes on them, seeing something beautiful in
them, in that brilliant radiance, something magical,
changes, new things, to distract her from that little
carriage that aged more each day, more and more,
becoming coated with dust. How pretty! And the

doctor bills. The little blanket getting so threadbare, the green beginning to fade under the sun. And her husband? Irritable last night. Playing the old Grundig at full blast. Medicine, distraction, medicine to quiet the child's wailing, the wailing... But, yet, sometimes... If the pea soup was good and hot and the meat nice and lean and not too rare, he would amuse her afterwards. A bit of gossip from the Palace. Involving that Jack Peurifoy maybe. Would he stay angry at the President? Did he really have the power? To carry out his threats? Why hasn't Arbenz told him to go to hell? Would he like him better if he grew a mustache? Oh, that husband of hers, always inventing things. Going on about land reforms, fruit companies, and threats. And he'd smile that sly smile of his as he affectionately patted his navel, his big pupils dilated wide. He was a good husband. Even though he drank. The pain of the allergic child. It hurt her, too, but she didn't. The thing is that men.... From the moment he left the office, the hands of the cathedral clock marking six on the dot as he entered the Bar Madrid shouting *Viva Euzkadi!* and then working his way home drink by drink. Around seven, the knock on the door, then the whistling if she didn't make it quick, and getting a funereal kiss along with his bad breath, his sharp whiskers pricking her lips, jacket over his shoulder, necktie halfway down his chest. Is dinner ready?

So long, old girl. See you tonight.

The silvery dust against the clouds. As impassive as the vultures with which they shared the sky. And she watched them grow, grow, like soap bubbles, like illustrations in a fairy tale book. She remembered that she hadn't turned the beans. And the squeaking of the little carriage. It broke up her daydream. She raised the hood. The hives had erupted again. She picked him up, *ay, mi baby, mi baby,* with no signs of tears on her stony face. His little arms around her neck, scratching her. Those little hands, cool skin, sweaty. When his breathing sounded more normal she put him back under the little green blanket. The distant sound of the cathedral clock striking four exploded the silence, startling the magpies. Four o'clock on the dot. She worried about being late at the doctor's office, it was still several blocks away. Overhead, the sound of planes grew louder, gradually, slowly. A few more blocks still to go, quite a distance to cover without a rest. And she kept pushing the little carriage anxiously. It reminded her of her oldest nephew, crazy about planes, who could tell you what kind it was at any distance by the sound alone. He was going to be a pilot for sure when he grew up and she would tremble every time he went up. And he'd influence her son, her little baby. Something would have to be done to redirect the boy's leanings. And then they started, the sirens, the sirens. A couple crossing the street thought it was an ambulance, some kids zigzagging by spoke of fire engines. But no smoke was to be seen in the sky. An accident? There were no cries or screeching of brakes. Somebody run over? Rescue operation? False alarm? She imagined the ambulance with a great red cross in the middle skimming down the hill on the way to save another life. The baby whimpered and she continued on her way.

The first bomb exploded in the northwestern part of the city. She raised her eyes. A blinding flash. Couldn't be rain. And then the earth shook and she felt as though she was losing her balance. Earthquake! she shouted. An earthquake! But then she heard the guffaw of the plane.

For she knew all those stories so well. How Xelajú had been destroyed at the turn of the century. Buried alive by the raging ashes of the Santa María, mocked by the thunder of little Santiago. Her mother had told her about it so many times. How her father, still a baby at the time, was saved by an absolute miracle. He was asleep when it began to quake. An uncle snatched him out of his cradle just as the roof was caving in on top of him. They rushed out to the open, desolate countryside just in time to see the Santa María explode and melt the sky. Then they moved to the city. The little they managed to save was thrown onto an ox cart. Then it was a matter of taking turns pulling, pulling, pulling the 200 kilometers to the city. All the oxen were of course dead. Their house was dead. Like all the others. Engulfed by a great wave of ashes. They built a new house in the capital, everybody working, everybody helping, and when it was finished they all watched it collapse on that famous Christmas Eve of 1917 when God shook the earth to arouse the people. It was time to march against Estrada Cabrera. And her parents, yes, they helped clean up too. Just like she did in 1944. Another dictatorship, another revolution. As deathless as the volcanoes themselves, old patriarchs annoyed by the mean-tempered sound of the plane that climbed, gleaming whitely from cloud to cloud.

As constant and recurring as Katún 8 Ahau of the Mayan long count. Peurifoy had kept his word.

The explosion shook the whole world. Ladies and top-hatted gentlemen carrying umbrellas came tumbling downhill. A chewing-gum vendor was seen rolling by followed by a little white dog with long ears. Then a shoeshine boy leaving a long trail of coins that spilled from his box. A wooden leg flashed by and a half-eaten melon. A set of false teeth rolled down the hill, a woman right behind green with embarrassment, covering her mouth with her hands. A cloud of fine gray dust began to settle over everything right after the explosion of the second bomb further to the south. She was barely able to keep her balance after the first. The second knocked her to the ground. She fell and skinned her knees on the rough cement. Another pair of my *Schiaparellis* ruined! when the third exploded. But her husband insisted that *No Nonsense* weren't good enough for her. The next explosion tore the rattle off the carriage that was lifted one, two, three inches from the ground, threatening to fly away with her baby and she jumped to catch it. Her back, arms, and legs now coated thinly with gray dust. She was untying the ribbons that held his little arms in check, as a chunk of bread struck her in the face and an acquaintance, somersaulting by, waved. She took the baby out of the carriage and wrapped him with her sweater close to her heart. The facade of the building on the corner collapsed and where, where could she run? Where hide? The baby began to cry and the first flames appeared on the roofs. The sky grew black, the smoke thickened to the northeast and the south. As she pressed him against her she felt the pustules bursting, the wetness of the pus. And she began to run. She could still see the carriage with the parrot-green little blanket start rolling down the hill, slowly at first, slowly, then gaining momentum, the little carriage that had served three generations so loyally, careening out of sight in the distance on the Street of Sighs, bouncing on its way to the rhythm of the explosions as it went by the Avenue of Freedom without stopping and then further on, and further, faster, another explosion, a two-story house collapsing on her left, the heavy brown air stifling her lungs, and the little carriage further and further down, passing the Avenue of Desire and the Street of Hope, rolling fast, rolling wildly, the fires growing and the sky in darkness. Rolling along the Avenue of Emptiness, smaller and smaller, rolling, going forever, rolling, goodbye, far away, smaller still, the little family carriage, goodbye, until nothing remained of it but a tiny silver dot gleaming in the distance.

It had taken her hours to get home. Was it hours? It was. The infant was gasping, agitated, sweating, and that smell of pus. The air swollen with dust and smoke and looking up into the sky from the front door, in her sad patio the daisies, the thick carnations, and those lush begonias, the cages of singing canaries and multicolored parakeets hanging at the entranceway, and the horsetail ferns in every corner all becoming enveloped in blanket of gray, reminding her of the morning she had been awakened to discover the rain of ashes, the ashes of Fuego volcano, that morning in 1944. Now, the whistling dive of the plane piercing a million ears, her eyes closed anticipating the explosion to ensue.

15

Dust, dust, pouring from every corner, the quaking, the flower pots crashing to the ground, the windows bursting, dust. Old dust, witness to generations. She saw a pair of mice leave the house and scurry across the patio to the safety of the rear wall. She saw cockroaches fleeing over the roofs and spiders weeping in despair. The cages bouncing crazily in all directions banging against one another, the little birds frantic, beating their wings, breathless, cutting their wings on the cold metal, their feathers falling. She ran towards the cages, the infant in her arms, and opened the doors with her free hand. Go, go! She had watched them being born. Children of the children of the children of her grandmother's birds. She had raised them. They were hers. But this was the end of them.

She ran to the kitchen for the baby's bottle and returned to the study. A huge mahogany desk stood in the center, her grandfather's old desk. Massive. Serene. She pulled the chair away and squeezed under the desk. The baby was crying. He was hot and gasping. But she felt safe under the desk. She tried to yell but heard only the silence. Her ears shattered by the booming echoes of bomb after bomb, blinding flashes in the empty darkness, the earth trembling. She began to pray. In a monotone, words in Latin she had never understood. She tried to calm the baby. She scanned his face. In her distraction, yes, she had forgotten those little unrestrained arms. He had scratched. Scouring his fists against his skin trying to relieve the itching. Now, those pits again, blood running from his chocolate cheeks, trickling down his plump little chin. She reached for a couple of pencils on the desk and a roll of gauze in one of the drawers. She made them into splints over the elbows, tight. Outside, another bomb. And asking herself what could be happening to her husband. He would have been in his office, second floor, to the right, the National Palace. Would they dare bomb the National Palace? He'd be cracking jokes, maybe, with the other employees, his jacket off, shirt half-wrinkled. It would almost surely be his latest about Mr. Peurifoy. Or maybe he'd be doing his imitation of Mr. Foster Suck's face while listening to Señor Toriello's speech at the last meeting of the Organization of American Colonies. Possibly they didn't even pay attention to the planes until very late on. The first explosion must have sent him to the floor. Hopefully he didn't bang his hip when he fell. If he hurt that hip again, with all the baby was costing. And the Minister. What if he fell down, too? He had one leg shorter than the other. Would he have been able to get up again?

So long, old girl. See you tonight.

Night fell but the bombing didn't stop. Neither the electricity nor her husband came back that night. She remained crouched under the great desk unable to quiet the baby, not with his bottle, nor his pacifier, nor songs she tried to sing that wouldn't come out. The baby stretching out his little arms, stiffened with the pair of Mongol #2's, his legs kicking less and less. It had been raining since afternoon. A June drizzle. She watched the droplets playing tag on the one window pane that remained intact. The others done for by the explosions. The bombs. They were as overwhelming as the winter floods, as the swollen rivers she remembered from when she was little, roaring down from the mountains, carrying along trees, rock, cows, houses, people, demolishing farms, swamping fields, cutting new channels, flattening hills, washing away bridges, tearing up highways and displacing trucks, the roaring waters regurgitating their rage, people fleeing in a terrified swarm, scampering for refuge impossible to find. The water covering everything.

A thin candle sputtered asthmatically in the middle of the room. Her only light. The Thunderbolts coming out of their dive, ready for the next, the sirens that didn't stop howling, sirens, sirens, and sporadic rat-a-tats followed by occasional single shots. And then, silence and cold. Was her husband fighting? They had first met under fire, after all. That distant 1944 when Ubico was brought down. He had been shot in the hip and couldn't stand without her help. That distant June. Where could he be now? Where? How was he? Was he all right? She recalled the classical national joke. Guatemala had declared war on Germany and Churchill hurried to his atlas to find out where the new ally was situated. Cigar in hand he pored over his maps. Nowhere to be found. Searching again more closely he brushed away a tiny little volcano of ashes fallen from his cigar. And there it was. Under the great man's ashes. The child, agitated, began to kick. My baby! She began to rock him in her arms. *Duerme si, duerme ya,* the old lullaby strained through her teeth between one flash and the next and the magma of sound that seemed no longer to touch her, no longer to disturb her. What to do? The plaster falling all around her. And glass everywhere. She could clearly hear the old dinner service smashing in the kitchen, her mother's fine old china with the rose designs dying one by one. And more plaster. The whole house coming down! The candle struggling to keep alight, the infant's breast heaving up, down, up, the choking dust rising, the last group of mice fleeing the room. She needed her husband!

CHAPTER 2

FUNERAL
FOR A BIRD

As soon as the bombing ended a new government was in. The distinguished man of arms, Colonel Castle Cannons, was in the Big Chair. But the people stayed in hiding. The great colonel had been lifted into power by the first explosion right after he completed the long marathon from Fort Leavenworth in the wheatfield state of Kansas, covering the full distance in purple trunks and checkered socks. Upon reaching the palace he found the Big Chair adrift. Not losing a beat he jumped into it, shouting "If you can't take the heat, you won't hold your seat." He settled back, comfortably, holes in the socks and all. After recovering his breath, he immediately ascended to the presidential balcony to explain to the people why bombing was necessary for the country's progress. The days went by and he continued preaching against the horrors posed by the enemies of democracy. He delivered his sermons from dawn till dusk with a two-hour break for lunch between twelve and two. And he rested again in the evening, of course, seeking respite from the arduous duties of the presidency at the Archbishop's Palace. Inevitably, rumor ran rife but nothing concrete ever came out.

Naturally, no one came to hear him speak. Sometimes, however, the Archbishop would sun himself at the fountain in the square licking his lollipop and applauding politely. The colonel leveled a long forefinger at invisible enemies whom he accused of treason against the democratic ideals of the tiny great nation. It was the same forefinger with which he ordered the sexton of the cathedral to be executed. Because — some said — while the sexton was sweeping the square one morning as he listened to the speech, he suddenly turned and yelled at him wanting to know why he didn't shut up and do something about clearing away the rubble from the city and letting the survivors out into the sunshine. But others claimed he did it for personal reasons.

One rather brisk morning, the servants out buying the bread could see in the distance the small figure that had been gesticulating so energetically falling from the balcony. Falling, falling, falling. Some said that the crash caused an earthquake in Japan. Others said that sainted Brother Pedro, who long ago cared for the poor, had appeared to the Archbishop. The only certainty is that when the long-suffering Mr. Foster Sucks imparted the tragic news to his president, the general, the latter uttered the now celebrated words, "What castle did you say lost its cannons?"

And a junta of three blue-blooded gentlemen assumed the task of keeping the seat polished until a successor could be elected.

The people began to emerge from their hiding places. From behind a door. From under tables. Caves. From the Bridge of the Cows, and some forgotten roof. It had been a long time since they had been out in the sunshine and their bones and muscles ached. Stiff, stiff. Paralysis as a rule. They should play. They should exercise. So they might function once again. But. Who could have thought of it? Their minds were too rusty. They'd been too busy hiding, too busy surviving. Everything so dark for so long. All the power generators were dead. And so damp, so rainy, and the wind. The bombs had caused huge dust clouds that remained hanging over the horizon, green dust and yellow and red dust and black. They had been totally deprived of light and it had been so cold. All the bodies emerged from their hiding places blind and shriveled. Tremulous jaws in stark contrast with the long, glistening hair and nobody could bend their knees.

An old woman was the first thing the boy Máximo saw. She was huddled against the ruins of a colonial mansion clutching a bundle to her breast. Bouts of coughing wracked her body, swaying back and forth. Máximo went towards her. He coughed too. Like she did. She was the first living being he had seen other than his mother. He poked her in the ribs with his middle finger. They felt hard and dry and the old woman did not react. He poked harder. What else to do? Ah, there was a stick lying in the middle of the street. He picked it up and began to hit the old woman over the head with it.

Can I help you?

Her eyes were staring at something else. They hadn't turned towards him. Weren't looking at him as he was looking at her. Did they have pupils? He wasn't sure. She was so tall he couldn't know for sure.

Can I help you?

Proud of himself. He was talking. He was talking to a stranger. He had never done that before. Only to his mother. And to his own reflection in the broken mirror he had found in the dust. But now. He felt proud. Except that she didn't speak back to him. His mother always answered him. Could it be a different kind of animal that didn't answer? He wanted very much for her to answer him.

Talk!

And he hit her on the head again. His mother always hit him on the head when he didn't pay attention. Not with a stick. But she had great big knuckles.

The bombs. The bombs have stopped.

She was talking. And sobbing, too. Was she sobbing? Dry sobs, more silence than sobs. More whimpers than sobs. Her mouth open, a huge cavern. He could fit into it for sure. But she had stopped speaking! He wanted more words. She had left her mouth open making a perfect circle but nothing more was coming out of it. He hit her again.

The bombs. The bombs have stopped.

He already knew that. He knew what bombs were. His mother had shown him. Dropping gently from the sky like feathers and about the size of a thumb. And she was right. They had stopped. He hadn't seen any for days now. Maybe months. Maybe even years. Did it make any difference? He couldn't remember the last time he'd seen one. But for sure, for sure, not this day. No. If it had been this day he wouldn't have been able come out. It had to have been some other day. Yes. The bombs had stopped. His mother had said that very same thing, now he remembered. The bombs had stopped. And when she came out from under the big desk and couldn't stand up straight he had laughed. Yes, she had looked funny bent over like that. But she had turned around and smacked him in the face. But when had that been, when?

I miss the bombs.

She missed the bombs! The old woman missed the bombs! But his mother had told him the bombs were bad. Did she know better? Worse than bad! That's what they were. His mother cursing them every day, every night, from the safety of the desk, fist clenched, venting her rage against the echo of the half-collapsed wall, in the name of blood and earth and then quivering with the explosions, *ayayayay Jesús*, with fear at each flash, *ayayayay mamita* but once over, again defying, again cursing and hating, and swearing that some day. When she wasn't looking he had tried to imitate her but he couldn't very well. The light will come on again when the bombs stop. She had said so over and over. The light. And now they had stopped. So why did she miss the bombs?

Because they were there.

Yes, he knew that, too. Things were there sometimes. His desk was there. He lived under it. His pacifier was there, too. In his mouth. And his mother. She, too. A little bent over. And the house, all smashed. The columns. The patio. So much dust and dirt. All that was there. And the piles of glass shards, were there, the chunks of wall, and the dead trees. So much there. The stones and those old dusty magazines. The sink and laundry tub. The charcoal range. The charcoal bin. The entranceway. The gutters. Yes, a lot of things were there.

It's painful. To lose something. That one. Is used to. Painful. Habit. Like with men. I loved my husband. He drank. There were better ones. But he was my husband. Changes are annoying. I would have been happy if the bombs had never fallen. But they fell. And the houses collapsed and nobody could stop it. I got used to it. Used to living with them. They fell every day at the same times. Their regularity made them understandable. It became so normal. To wake up real early and see the bombs dropping through the soft, fresh air. One knew where one stood and what to expect. But now they've stopped. We have to wait for something new. Something unknown again. And try to get used to it. No sooner are we comfortable with whatever comes our way than it's over, and something else will happen. What a mess!

She talked so much. At first she couldn't. Then only a little. And suddenly. People are so funny. Too bad he couldn't understand. She spoke such strange things and so fast. He had learned. If people talked too much you stopped understanding. You had to be careful about what you said. The old woman wasn't. With her, it was impossible. And with all the things he wanted to see, so many, a lot of things to see. He walked away from the old woman.

He wanted to see all the things his mother had told him about. He wanted to see the elephants in the spider web on the wall, and the fountain with the water that got small and got tall. It all had to be there in some street. Everything had to be on a street somewhere. His mother had told him about streets. Streets were where the houses didn't grow. He was walking on one. Looking for that fountain. He wanted to tell the little fountain his name. He knew his name. That was something else his mother had told him. His name was Máximo Sánchez. And if anybody said his name he knew they were talking to him. That's how easy it was. He knew how old he was, too. He knew so much already! He was nearly five. Four and a half, actually, but he felt older when he said nearly five. And he had scars on his face. His scars were pink. He could see them in the broken mirror. They were mostly on his cheeks and forehead. They were the scars of something called hives. Everything had its own name. He had to learn the names of a lot of things. Especially now that he could go outside. To the street. Street is what they call where he was now. It was narrow and dark and zigzagged between the ruins of the houses. And there were bodies everywhere. They didn't move. They were called corpses. And his mother had told him not to touch them. You got sick if you touched them. They were full of worms and worms were bad. He had asked his mother if he was full of worms, too, but she said only corpses. Poor little corpses! It was too bad they were dead. He couldn't play with them. Even though they really stank. He couldn't stand the smell. They deserved to die for smelling so bad. They made him feel sick to his stomach but he didn't want to vomit. Although he liked to see the confetti come out of his mouth he didn't like the taste. He kept walking with one hand over his nose and the other over his stomach. What about his father? Would he smell like that, too? No! His father wouldn't stink. He wasn't dead, anyway. Just alone maybe. He was disappeared. That's what his mother had told him. Maybe he would come home now that the bombs had stopped and the colonel had fallen off the balcony. His father would never smell like that. He had a very nice mustache. Will you be back soon, papa? Soon? When? When? Tell me if you're coming back!

He could go on in any direction. Walk on any street. That's what's called freedom. Sure, unless the street was blocked by fallen walls or piles of corpses. He wanted to walk on another street that didn't smell so bad. Too bad all the streets were blocked by fallen walls and piles of corpses. There wasn't much freedom. He lifted one leg, balancing himself carefully on the other, arms spread out to help him, and took a big leap, jumping over a puddle of blood in the middle of the street. Every once in a while there was a puddle of blood in the middle of the street. But it was possible to do everything. To fly, float, fool around, run here, run there, keep running all the time. He was free.

And it began to rain. Lightly at first. One drop after another, with quite a while between drops. He could stick out his tongue and try to taste them, what yummy drops, but taking care that no fleas or lice got into his mouth. He could feel each drop caress his hair. Feel the bounce going right down into the middle of his head like a drowsy sigh. He liked the rain. He could see the drops of water burst against the remains of the old walls. He also knew that they were old walls. His mother had told him. The drops took up the colors which would shine again inside each drop, bright colors, and the drops carried them along crossing and crisscrossing with one another everywhere in shades of red and blue or yellow, all colors, all running along until they reached the gray dust on the ground and then running along the dust itself making rainbow furrows like a spreading spider web. Where was the fountain with the water that got tall and got small? And the drops fell faster, stronger, more violently, falling without stopping, falling, taking up all the colors until the wall began to be white all over, the colors fleeing furiously through the furrows until they could hide under the dust.

He got wet and began to feel cold. His clothes were sticking to him. His skin was full of tiny bumps. But those weren't hives. They were called goose pimples. And the last colors ran very fast, the sky was solid gray. He began chasing the colors, running along a street where he noticed dark blue tones and crossed where bright reds were slipping by, and down another street after some shy violets. And he ran, street after zigzagging street, crossing to the right, the left, the rain even stronger, ruins bigger, the cold, a little group of mutilated corpses smiling, the cold, columns and old doors scattered on the street, the cold. All the corpses had their mouths open. He didn't want them snapping at his heels. His mother had told him they couldn't move but he wasn't so sure. He watched a cockroach scurry out of one of the open mouths. Did they all get born inside the dead person? How did they know when it was time for them to get born? And then something solid hit him on the forehead, bounced to the ground before him, and got lost in the mud. A bomb? He bent over to look for it. He found it. It was cold. Like a piece of glass and it turned to water in hand. More and more things like that began falling all around. Big ones, little ones. He didn't know their names. Another one hit him on the shoulder. A bigger one. And more came. He had to find a hiding place. More came. And the cold. It was never cold under the old desk. His mother would be waiting there for him with her white hair and toothless mouth. Would she still be bent over? Maybe he should go back. And another one hit him. And he still didn't know its name. Should he go back, maybe?

There it is! Hey, look, everybody!

He was in a place where he had never been before. A very narrow alley. And in the center of it was a dead bird. Children of all sizes came running out of the neighboring ruins. He wasn't the only one, then. Of all sizes, and brave, not going home in spite of the cold. Some were his size. They looked a little like him in the broken mirror. And there were bigger children. All were shouting, pointing.

A dead bird! A dead bird!

He had never seen a dead bird before. Nor a live one. Just photos of birds in the old magazines in his house. He looked at them all the time. He could remember all the pictures. There wasn't much to do under the old desk. But this bird, his bird. It looked like all the photos he had seen. The general shape, anyway. Smaller than he had imagined. He had thought about them so much, so much, crossing the sky, making no sound, with bombs under their wings. This was a very little one.

A dead bird! A dead bird!

And all the children ran towards it. And he. He ran, too, very excited. He did not see the headless body that lay behind the small pile of moldy bricks. He tripped over it. A belly-whopper right in the mud. A speck of dirt got into his left eye. He stood up. He wiped his hands and brushed off his trousers. He did not cry. His arms were scratched. He could see the droplets of blood, so red. In a fit of anger, he began kicking the body. His foot went halfway into it as though it were a sack of cotton. A bump came out at the back that disappeared when the pressure came off. Corpses! Corpses all over the place! But then he remembered the bird.

Look at it, everybody!

All the children surrounded the dead bird and more and more kept coming. Pretty soon there were ten. Then fifteen, maybe twenty. Maybe more. The oldest boy made sure nobody got too close. They might damage it. Watch out there! Not so close! Don't go stepping on it! Dummoxes! Then, no more came. The oldest boy dropped his arms and knelt before the tiny body. Dead silence in the group. The shortest ones slipped through to the front. Sighs and whispers. Poor bird! One of the littlest began to cry, very softly. But he wouldn't do that, no. The oldest boy remained kneeling before the body. Slowly he lowered his hand, ghostlike, bringing it down in slow motion until it touched the little body. He shuddered. Whispers. Then he stretched out his middle finger to stroke the breast. The whispering

31

grew louder. Somebody elbowed one of the smaller children in the nose. Máximo felt a pain in his foot. Some one was stepping on it but at that moment only the bird mattered. He didn't complain. The feathers are nice and soft, the oldest boy said. Poor bird. Let us touch it, too. No. It would all fall to pieces. It's little body is so frail. Poor bird. It had such a round little breast covered with down that was soft and white as raindrops. Its wings shut tight encircling the whole body as though protecting it from the cold. The neck was long, almost too long. The head at the end of it with a big black eye bulging out and the beak open. The feet very stiff sticking straight up. Do you think the hail killed it? No. There's no sign it was hit. It's possible, though. When something hits, it leaves a mark. Look at the bombs. But that's different. They explode. What's different about it? They kill, don't they? Yes, but they kill different. Maybe it broke its neck. Maybe. But something must have hit it. The hail couldn't have broken its neck. Why not? It's so small. A bomb could have broken it. But that's different. Shut up, said the oldest. Maybe it died of old age. No, man, nothing dies of old age. Everything dies of something. The oldest boy raised his arms commanding attention from the group. Conversation began to die away. What disrespect! Don't you see it's dead? He fixed his gaze on all those little pairs of eyes that one by one turned away. He bent down. Carefully he took the bird's head between thumb and forefinger, lifting it a little. Everybody bent over to see better. Poor bird. The neck looks okay. Maybe it cracked its head open. The hail might have done it. Several nodded. What should we do with it? The oldest boy smiled. He already knew what had to be done. Well, we can't just leave it here. People would step on it. They'd kick it. Dogs might eat it, maybe. We have to bury it. Sure, everybody shouted. The bird has to be buried. Poor bird. Máximo thought that it was a really pretty bird. Like those colors that ran away from the dead walls. Birds are good. Soft feathers, and so frail.

Everyone ran towards the rubble to find things for the funeral. Máximo didn't know what to look for. He had never been to a funeral. Nor heard anyone speak of one. Nor seen photos. What could a funeral be? Bring pretty things, the oldest boy had said. But the colors couldn't be brought. He'd have to look for something else, something that glittered. He went to the ruin closest by and began to poke around in the mud and among the shattered bricks.

Pretty things. I want only pretty things.

One of the children brought a board. Another brought scraps of different colored cloths. One of the little ones found a picture of a rose. A tall freckle-faced boy was ringing a little silver bell. Somebody had tallow candles. There was a watch. A plastic slipper. An air force medal. Two panties. A golden crucifix with arms and legs but no body. A yellowed laundry ticket. Máximo was the last to return. I found a ring, he shouted. A beautiful ring. The circle of children opened to make way for him to come through and place his offering at the dead bird's feet. He was proud of his find. And it really was beautiful. Solid gold with a gorgeous aquamarine in the middle. It was beautiful even with the finger inside it.

It's a woman's. Look at the nail. Could be. But it has no nail polish. Some women don't use polish, my mother never does. Maybe she didn't have any left. Maybe the explosion burned off the polish. Maybe it's a man's with long nails. Maybe it's a Martian's finger, it's kind of green. No, that's because it's rotting. It's not rotting, it's just half-burned, if it was rotting it would stink. Do you call that a nice smell? But it would be worse. Didn't you ever smell a corpse before?

Okay, enough, said the oldest. The bird has to be buried. Does everybody agree? Okay. Put the board next to the bird. No, not like that, closer, and careful you don't get mud all over it. Okay. I know, I know, so's it won't get all muddy. Okay. Now, move back, I'm going to pick up the body. He knelt again as the heads all sought a better vantage point. His hands curved around the bird, lifted it, the head hanging to one side, bobbing in the air out of control. He put it on the board rearranging the head in its original position. Some applauded. Okay. Now, you, cover it with that cloth there. No. Better the other. Yes, that one. And let's put the medal above the head. Like that. Like a dead pilot. And the ring at its feet. Sure, finger and all. It's the owner's finger, isn't it?

The freckle-faced boy with the little bell led the procession. Stopping at every corner, shaking the little bell in the air and shouting, a dead bird! In all four directions, a dead bird! At every corner. A column of pious children following, trying hard to keep a straight face. Some were carrying candles. Those who weren't pretended to be. Behind them, the photograph of the rose, high in the air so that all could see it. Next, came the panties on the ends of a couple of sticks, and the the golden crucifix without a body. After them, the board with the remains. It rode on the shoulders of six boys, three on a side, the bigger ones. Swerving solemnly from one side of the street to the other, in imminent danger of falling. Behind, the smallest ones, trotting along behind. Máximo among them. And it kept on raining. But the bird was dead. It had to be buried. It had to be buried, the bird was dead. And it rained and rained and rained.

They reached an intersection where there had been an empty lot. The oldest boy decided that it was the right place. The smaller ones were ordered to begin working digging a hole. With a variety of sticks. With the plastic slipper. With an old broom. It wasn't very hard. The soft, moist earth, lumps of mud flying every which way. In practically no time they had dug a large enough hole.

The panties were laid down at the bottom. On top of them, the photo of the rose, face up. And then the board with the body and the beautiful decorations. All in a circle around the hole, eyes fixed on the inert feathery body. Only the murmuring of the rain was to be heard. Everything had stopped. They didn't move, didn't speak. Just contemplating the little creature, the stiff legs. The oldest boy took the crucifix and let it fall on the body. Okay. Now cover it up. All at the same time, kneeling in the mud, shoveling in an unspoken competition each trying to outdo the others. Nobody noticed the old man approaching.

Hey, you boys there, what are you up to?

Everyone turned. Máximo saw how his black overcoat dragged in the mud. He was bowlegged. One leg, almost useless, dragged after the other, the old man propping himself up with a stick of wood.

His long dirty-gray beard had mud on it and scraps of food. His chalky skin covered with sores, especially around his broad nose. His slack jaw never stopped wagging from side to side.

What are you doing, I said!

They stood where they were, frozen, paralyzed, what to do? Protecting their secret, what to do? The littlest boy began to cry. Seeing this, one of the others ran off. Another followed in his tracks. And another. Very soon it was a mass exodus, stepping on one another, pushing elbowing, scratching, all scrambling to get away as fast as they could.

Don't run away! Don't run away, I say! I want to know what you're up to, that's all. You don't have to run away!

Máximo was the only one left. The old man puzzled him. Could that be his father? Would his father look like that? No. the old man had no mustache. A father without a mustache? No. Impossible that the old man could be his father if he had no mustache. The mustache was his father. What one always noticed in the photos. What his mother always mentioned. The gringos have no mustaches but your father does. That's what she said. But why did all the others run away? The shaky hands? The twisted, dried-up legs? The hairy ears? What made them run away? And he? Should he run, too? Would he be able to? And what if he couldn't? If all the old man wanted was just to talk. Why be afraid? Those eyes that were so red? The dried snot beneath his nose?

You, brave guy, come over here.

He was talking to him. The man was talking to him.

Come over here. This old man couldn't do anything to you even if he wanted to. Come on.

I have to go home. My mother is waiting for me under the desk.

You're afraid of me, aren't you, you rascal. But, it's all right, sonny, this old man won't hurt you.

Could I? No? He lifted one foot. Could I? What? He put it down a couple of inches ahead. Could I? Yes? He lifted the other foot. I can.

You're the brave one of the bunch, you are.

I've got to get going now.

Rascals! By my grandmother's bones! Big shots when they're alone but as soon as somebody comes along, like me, they run like rabbits to hide in the ruins. Look at them! There they go! Like rats scurrying around corners. Over there, look, on Street of Illusions and Street of Sighs. Just look!

Máximo looked. But the words that man was saying. Street of Illusions. Street of Sighs. Streets had names, too, like people. All he had to know was the name of each street. And he'd be able to talk about them. He'd be able to name them. Names and words. So much to learn. By my grandmother's bones! Tell me, sonny. What were you all doing here? And watch out about telling lies, hear, or I'll give your ears a pull you won't forget.

A bird died. We were burying it.

A bird?

Yes. With little white feathers on its chest.

A bird! How about that! And where did you find a bird?

On that street.

Street of Sighs.

Yes. That one. It was dead. Right out in the street. We couldn't leave it there.

No, no. Absolutely not.

Someone would have stepped on it. It was very little and so soft.

Yes, birds are generally like that.

And so we decided to bury it. Over there.

Now I see. That's what you were all doing. And could you tell me just how you went about burying it?

With dirt. We dug a hole and we put it inside. Then we covered it over.

And that's all? Didn't you put in something along with it to protect it from the cold?

Yes. Yes. We made a procession. It went on a board and the big boys carried it. I walked behind. But I was carrying my ring. The ring I found for it.

And what else?

It was covered over and had a gold medal. This big.

Fine, you did a very good thing. But the poor bird. You didn't bury it properly.

No?

It wasn't your fault, of course. I'm sure none of you ever had any experience in this business of the dead. But let me go on. You should have burned incense when you had the bird on the board. And then sprinkled the body with petals of flowers for the dead and few drops of *Indita*. That helps the soul along on its trip to the other world. Of course the way things are now, there's no place to get any. In any case, one has to improvise. But. Oh. Yes. Something very important. When the board was lifted up, you should have circled around three full turns to the right and four to the left. Seven in all. To confuse the soul so it can't come back to this life of poverty and suffering. Imagine if the poor thing had to come back and live through it all over again. Naturally, you didn't know. So, don't feel bad about it. You did your best. It doesn't matter. It doesn't matter, I said.

Flowers and incense and seven circles to confuse the soul? He was confused. He did the same as everyone else. What he was told. Burying the bird would never have occurred to him alone. He didn't even know that things had to be buried. What was incense? *Indita*? What's a soul? He noticed several shiny leaves with fine thorns stuck to the old man's shoes.

Don't you agree? The old man opened his mouth to laugh even though nothing came out. He took a step forward to pat his head. The boy drew back. The old man made an effort to change direction at the last moment and lost his balance. He began to flail about in a desperate attempt to keep on his feet. Máximo quickly stretched out his hand to him. The old man righted himself, squeezing his hand tightly for a long moment as he caught his breath. His breathing was labored. Máximo saw that there were many dead leaves rotting in the mud.

By my grandmother's bones! And me beginning to think that dead birds was all that mattered to you.

No. But I have to go now.

Such impatience! My goodness! Are you by any chance going to Street of Sighs? You don't know which it is? That one, see, that one. Isn't that the way you're going? You are, aren't you? Just as I thought. Fine. It so happens I'm going that way, too. Will you come along with me as far as your house? I could lean on your shoulder and it'll be easier to walk. What do you say?

Máximo wasn't sure. Could he trust the old man? He was cold again. And hungry. Would it take very long?

They walked side by side along deserted streets, heaps of broken glass below the balustrades. Máximo wiped his nose with his free hand. Not a single house had gone undamaged. The rain obscured the afternoon. There wasn't a single bird in the whole sky. Only the mist slinking through the openings of the ruins. Máximo asked the old man where he was going.

Oh, sonny. On the way to nowhere. In no direction. You don't get me, do you? Well, it's hard to understand, I know. I'm just going along, anywhere at all, no, not to any house, not to any place. You still don't catch on? Well, forget it. Let me tell you a story instead. Did you ever hear the story of Tecún Umán?

No. I've lived under a desk my whole life and my mother lost her teeth.

All right, then. I'll tell it to you. It's a very old story. It's told to everybody, sooner or later. Some day you'll be bored hearing it so often, you'll see. Did it happen for real? What difference does it make? All that matters is whether it's a good story or not. If you get bored, then it's no good. And so. Here goes. Now be quiet. The Spaniards invaded this land way back when, before there were bombs. Yes, it was a long time ago. By my grandmother's bones, let me get on with the story. They had shotguns and horses. And a handful of people they picked up in Mexico. What

40

the devil could those poor Indians do? But they weren't going to stand around scratching themselves, either. No, siree! Nothing of the kind. Here we bust our guts, they said. And the Quichés were the toughest of them all. There were a lot of tribes. Like twelve. Maybe more. But the Quichés were tops. They didn't fool around. And Tecún was their lord. Their prince. What do you mean, what Tecún? Tecún Umán, man! Didn't I say I was going to tell you his story? The rain's soaked into your skull, man. Let me get on with the story. Tecún already was a legend then. Outstanding. A strapping, good-looking fellow, the kind that makes the girls see blue spots in front of their eyes. Now, then. The Spaniards kept on beating their chests, making trouble, sticking their noses into everything. They went around saying that God sent them. The Spaniards have always put everything off on God. Be that as it may. Tecún decided that the time had come to stop this nonsense, they weren't going to put up with it any more. They were going to have it out on the Xelajú plains. And his princess, a real pretty little thing, too, was named Alxit. And when she found out about Tecún's plans, she had a fit. So, you're walking out on me, you don't love me, you're selfish and inconsiderate, the first chance you get, off you go, and all those things women are always saying. And he, well, what can I do, it's not for nothing I'm prince, I can't be standing around watching how those gringos keep grabbing off more and more and, think about it, I'm also going on your account because Kukulkán only knows what they'll to do to you if they ever lay hands on you. And he gave her a whole lecture and there was nothing the

41

princess could do anymore but say *ciao* to him. And Tecún set out that February and met up with the Spaniards on the Pacajá plateau, south of Xelajú, where they were on an outing, a *picnic*, as they call it. Well, now, he said to them, what's all this about having an outing on land that doesn't belong to you, *Señores gringos*? Look at all the garbage you're making. Chicken bones everywhere. And all those empty bottles there, just look. The Spaniards went running for their muskets and the priest, all sweated up, raised the cross and cussed them out in Latin. *Señor cura*, Tecún, said. That thing is made of national lumber and you haven't paid the export duty. Would you be so good as to cough up? You have offended the holy and illustrious name of our Lord Jesus Christ, shouted the priest. Finish them off, my stalwarts. And the battle started. They were at each other's throats all day long and by afternoon it seemed that the Spaniards were beginning to win. After all, they had the gunpowder and the horses, which were neighing like crazy, and so the situation looked pretty bad for Tecún. But what could he do? He wasn't about to go back home. Imagine what Alxit would say. He didn't want to even think. So, he held his breath, tightened his loin cloth, and forced his way through the Spanish cavalry until he stood gasping face to face with the Spanish captain. *Señor capitán*, said Tecún. You people could at least bathe more often, I had to hold my breath to be able to get over here. What you need are our steam baths. What's this *Señor capitán* business? the Spaniard responded. Tonadiú, if you don't mind, as all the savages call me. With the accent on the "u." It means blond-haired. Only a gringo could talk like that, said

Tecún, and let fly at him. Tonadiú was able to jump out of the way but his horse couldn't and Tecún ran him through with his spear, the point coming out under his tail. What a hell of a thing, you lousy Indian, now you've left me without a horse, the Spaniard said to him. Watch out you don't scratch my saddle, it's from Toledo. He was really a beauty, said Tecún, and he bent over to stroke him. Arab, I'll bet. Tonadiú took advantage of Tecún's lapse to plunge his sword into him in the same spot that the spear had come out of the horse. Ay, Kukulkán, I've been shafted yelled Tecún and fell over dead on top of the horse. And as soon as I find your Alxit, I'll shaft her, too, but from the front, yelled Tonadiú and, as he was raising his sword in triumph, he transfixed the quetzal through the breast that had flown down at that very instant to see whether its master was dead or only making believe. Now, I've let this buzzard have it, too, said Tonadiú, throwing the bird's body on top of Tecún's. And the battle was over. The drums began announcing the death of Tecún and the Quichés all went around with long faces. They argued and argued but couldn't decide what to do. Finally, the idea of the palace caretaker was accepted which was to send an emissary with gold and jewels to Xelajú to invite Tonadiú to the Quiché capital to discuss a surrender. Meanwhile, all the women and kids would be sent up into the mountain and they would pack the houses with straw. Then they would burn down the city during the night and make barbecue of the Spaniards. To sacrifice their capital so as to finish off the gringos. How about that? No letting yourself be subjugated and that kind of stuff. By my grandmother's bones!

Meanwhile, Alxit was going around out of her mind over Tecún's death. They've killed my man, what do I do now, he left me without a centavo, the usual thing. And they wanted to get her out of the city along with the others but stubborn as she was, she slipped away from them and went to Tojil's shrine where she burned incense all afternoon long. You, Tojil, don't let those gringo sons of the pope keep doing as they please and getting away with it, that isn't fair, and all the rest of the things that are said in private to Tojil. When it was dark, she went to the woods and set out for the tallest peak. She climbed all night long, up and up, feet do your stuff, not arriving at the top until daybreak. And then she plunged a poisoned knife into her heart, shouting, this is it, Tonadiú, you'll never take me alive, and made a sign with her fingers that wasn't the sign of the cross. And that's where the others found her, they were all proud of their princess, she had preferred to kill herself rather than be had by the Spaniards. And they buried her in that place. And to this day the Indians go there to talk to her in the same way she talked to Tojil. It is near the old road from Xelajú to Iximché. And the Spaniards never did find her body.

The old man stopped, pointed with his stick at an unusually colored stone in the street, and spit out a yellow gob of phlegm that landed neatly at the edge of a puddle.

And what about the Spaniards? Did they barbecue them?

Ah, no. They got away, the scoundrels. Some stool pigeon brought them word and, feet do your stuff, they skipped. The next day they returned and burned the city, the two kings along with the rest. A few managed to get away to Chichicastenango where they sat down to watch the flames. By my grandmothers bones! But let me tell you something. Some day, if you like, you can visit the place where Alxit is buried. It's at the peak of the mountain called María Tecún.

They walked on in silence. The old man began to cough and he squeezed Máximo's hand. The street was lined with piles of garbage. Papers tossed in the air by the evening breeze. It stank.

I like your story! What does it mean?

For goodness sake! It is what it is. Anything. Whatever you want.

Could it tell me where to find my father?

Who? The story?

Yes.

Maybe yes, maybe no.

I only want to know where he is.

The old man's stick almost got caught in the roots of some dead bushes. His red nose looked like a turkey's.

And it didn't tell me where you were going, either.

For goodness sake! You want everything spoon-fed. But it's not like that in stories. The truth isn't always a truth that you can see and touch. But remember. It's a truth, anyway, as great, if not greater, than any other truth.

I don't understand anything.

Doesn't matter. Just enjoy it. Enjoy the story just as a story. Don't you worry. You'll be hearing from your father. I'm sure of it. Now, don't be expecting to find him the first day you look, hear? Things never come out the first day.

He turned halfway around to look at an old couple holding hands under a dead tree. There were yellow tobacco stains on his beard and dried scraps of food clinging to it. The old man was shaken by a fit of coughing.

Are you sick?

Just tired, sonny. Just tired.

It was then that Máximo recognized his street. He let go of the old man's hand and ran, that old mahogany door with its gilt knocker. A lion's head holding a ring in its open mouth. His house. He turned around. The old man was beginning to draw away with only his stick to accompany him.

Hey! What about you? You never said.

The old man continued on his way. Máximo ran to him and tugged at his coat. The old man looked at him, mouth open in what seemed like a silent guffaw. Cleaning his yellow teeth with his long black nails.

I have to leave, sonny. It was a disappointment coming here. Not worth all the pain in the bones. I'm going, I'll leave the whole place to you. Bury all the birds you want. Well, the bombs have stopped.

A good thing. Maybe they'll begin all over again tomorrow. But me, I've had it. Let go, now. I don't have all day.

Máximo let go of him. He stood watching him, the old man drawing out of sight, limping rapidly away. The rain began to let up but enormous black clouds still hid the sun. Máximo followed the old man with his eyes. He didn't understand. So many, many questions unanswered. But it was a good story.

He had enjoyed it. He didn't get bored. Even though the good guys lost. Now he could tell it to his mother. And about the colors and about the bird. Now he had so much to tell. And maybe she had discovered meanwhile where his father was. He turned and ran toward the heavy door, kicking at all the stones in his path.

CHAPTER 3

BONFIRE

When Máximo entered third grade, a new government came to power. The event brought about such disruption that the schools were closed.

He still remembered when the elections were called. Not long after Colonel Castle Cannons fell off the balcony. The assassination of five of the candidates had caused some delay. Panic erupted when the news came out. Tranquility returned when it was known that the army candidates had miraculously survived. Smiles reappeared once again on the faces of the grateful populace. Reconstruction forged ahead.

The citizens went to the polls on a bright and cheery Sunday in March. Two generals and one *licenciado*, a retired lawyer, vied for the honor of occupying the Big Chair. The Archbishop was in the main square distributing balloons to the the children while their parents received instructions on which way to vote. The people were all smiles.

And the welcome news on the front page the next day. The *licenciado* had won. An alert was declared that same afternoon. The soldiers tore through the streets burning buses and demanding a recount. The people walked home from work wondering what to do. A state of siege was declared the third day. The Association of Night Club Proprietors marched on the National Palace to protest against the 9:00 p.m. curfew. The sidewalks were lined with whores applauding the demonstrators and making eyes at the policemen.

The main square was jammed. The acting president came out on the balcony. He shared their concern, he told them in his thirsty-camel voice, the whores daring him to come outside, and the Archbishop scowling. He would find a solution, the acting president promised.

Army trucks surrounded the square. Soldiers with machine guns filed out. Nobody move, shouted an officer through the loudspeakers. Everybody hands up. A toothless whore threw herself into the fountain. The soldiers began handcuffing everyone, hands behind their backs. If there's a sound out of anybody, no matter what, that'll be the end of him, the officer shouted through the loudspeakers. A crow began to screech from a tree top and it was the end of him. That'll show you, shouted the officer over the loudspeakers. Better not fool with me. The army says what it means and means what it says. All those handcuffed were taken to the trucks. The whores refusing to go unless they were paid and the Archbishop blushing. He held the sexton's hand, patting it listlessly. The square was cleared in five minutes. The Red Cross removed the crow's body, a photograph of which appeared on the front page of the newspapers the next day. The trucks dropped the whores off at the crazies' park and continued on their way to the airport where the C-47's were waiting, engines warming.

The sun was wreathed in clouds when the last body was loaded onto the plane. The first raindrops were already falling by the time it took off southward. Soon there was a downpour. It must have been about four o'clock when they opened the doors and dumped the bodies into the Pacific. Headfirst.

The students protested the murder of the crow. Meetings were held and solidarity committees formed. Demonstrations were planned. All the schools of the university closed down. Their deans resigned. The crow was embalmed and reappeared in the main hall of the Museum of Natural History.

One morning two weeks later the president-elect was found dead. It seems that a mouse had found its way into his mouth as he slept and got stuck in his throat. And unfortunate accident to one who would have made a great *Señor Presidente*. A minority of the population suspected stupid things but fortunately no formal complaints were made. New elections were scheduled for the first Sunday in November. The two surviving generals would dispute the honor of occupying the Big Chair.

There was little publicity and the curfew was extended to 10 p.m. It seems that order was finally restored and that the people had freely and peacefully chosen the democratic way. The acting president promised fireworks for the Independence Day celebration. A soccer team famous around the world was invited to entertain the crowds. A circus arrived. The Street of Sighs was completely rebuilt. By a week before elections not a single corpse remained on the streets.

The people turned out to vote that bright and cheery Sunday in November. The Archbishop was in the main square distributing balloons to the children while their parents received instructions on which way to vote. The people were all smiles.

And the horrifying news on the front page the next day. Nobody had won. Both candidates had tallied exactly the same number of votes, 213 1/2 each. An alert was declared that same afternoon. The soldiers tore through the streets burning buses and demanding a recount.

The people walked home from work wondering what to do. Someone suggested that illiterates should be given the vote. After all, they were the republic's great silent majority. That was precisely the problem, another replied. That they are the majority in the republic. Someone protested that if they wanted to vote why didn't they learn to read and write like everyone else. Another suggested that maybe the voting age should be dropped to 28 to allow students to vote. Someone answered that he belonged in Mexico or before a firing squad. That those were Communist ideas. It wasn't for nothing that they draw up those lists, it was said. We'll make sure your name gets on one of them, it was said. Someone suggested a lottery. Let Lady Luck be the one to pick our future leader. Another was in favor of holding a cockfight. It was well known that both generals owned the best fighting cocks in the whole isthmus. A cockfight, that was the republic's style. It had class. And without class life was not worth living.

It was on the front pages the next day. The tie would be broken by a duel. The following Sunday in the main square at five o'clock sharp in the morning with the Archbishop presiding over the ceremony. The two pistols for the event would be donated by the U.S. Ambassador who was to be one of the guests of honor. Soldiers worked day and night to erect the reviewing stand.

Sunday dawned clear and with no wind. The electrifying atmosphere permeating everything was comparable only to the nervous excitement at a Sunday soccer match between bitter rivals. All the guests of honor in morning dress and top hats arriving in magnificent carriages. Carriages because gasoline was reserved for the use of emergency vehicles: tanks, jeeps, and paddy wagons. Although a drum or two occasionally went to the fire fighters. A valiant effort on the government's part to stabilize an economy ravaged by the long stagnation that followed on the heels of the historic bombardment. The Carmelite nuns were invited to sing the national anthem from the cathedral balcony. Programs with large glossy color photographs of the contestants, their vital statistics, and soap and perfume advertisements were sold at the entrance to the stands. A Chinese magician was threading needles with his mouth while standing on one leg. The young man with a leather tricorne was selling reversible cubes invented by his 70-year-old mistress. A couple, paying no attention to the uproar was making love under a bedspread on the corner of the Avenue of Hope and the Street of Lies. The French

Ambassador noticed them as he passed by and tipped his hat. And then the cathedral bells began to ring. The time had come.

General Díaz, covered with medals, came from the Avenue of Hope. Two young cadets in dress uniform strode proudly behind him bearing a red velvet cushion on which a magnificent pistol lay. The general twirled his mustache before acknowledging the crowd's applause. He wore satin gloves and a quite thick monocle in his left eye.

General Nochez came from the Avenue of Fantasy smoking a huge cigar. Two beautiful whores in dress uniform strode proudly behind him bearing a blue velvet cushion on which a magnificent pistol lay. The general's big silver crucifix nearly fell off as he was acknowledging the crowd's applause. He removed his gloves and cape before he looked at his rival. The Archbishop shivered with emotion as the U.S. Ambassador whispered into his ear all the pertinent details on the magnificent pair of pistols. And citizens throughout the city were angrily pacing in their homes because of a last-minute decision not to broadcast the great duel on the Gillette Sports Cavalcade in order to avoid disorders that might prevent people from attending mass and making their weekly donations to Holy Mother Church. Military marches and Gregorian chants were broadcast instead. The people, dying to know who their new leader was going to be.

And the horrendous news on the front page the next day. Foreheads were beaded with sweat. Ears turned red and some coughed. Desperate sobs could be heard. Babies cried. Flowers died. The birds did not sing. The clouds did not lift. The Minister of Health reported an outbreak of stomach ulcers.

Both generals had scored a bullseye. Both fell. The nation's future was uncertain. Curfew was moved back to 8:00 p.m. The U.S. Ambassador was recalled to Washington for urgent consultation. Bus drivers went on strike. The Archbishop had a mild heart attack.

This was to have been Máximo's first year of school. But the government shut the schools because of the unrest, the strikes, and the disruption. The children were nevertheless all given credit for the year in recognition of their blamelessness. Máximo spent his free time taking arithmetic lessons from his mother. He learned to read and write and to spend the night in the living room watching the fire. She had a powerful baritone voice and liked to sing but refused to tell him stories.

Máximo would steal away to the roof. He enjoyed lying on the tiles and getting a slight tan as he watched the Air Force planes practice for future wars by shooting at passenger aircraft. But he was afraid his mother would find out. She was in mortal terror of bullets and lost her temper easily. He was certain he would get a good hiding if he was found out. How he enjoyed watching the vultures try to get away when chased, the sound of the motors, those invisible propellors merging with the blackish masses, feathers slowly falling, floating in the sky for a long time caressed like bombs by the breeze! And sometimes he thought of his father.

What had happened?

Something happened that had led to the bombardment. He knew that. And the bombs had changed everything. His father disappeared. The city destroyed. They'd turned the city upside down. That's what his mother said. He had to know. Who had bombed them? Why? They changed the color of the beans. The plums all rotted. Others now in the catbird seat. He would learn to read and write, add and subtract, and even multiply. But he already had the feeling that all he really wanted to learn was the answer to those questions, questions that had no answer. He bit on his pacifier. Close companion and adviser. But nobody would talk. Of the survivors, those who had not lost their heads lost their teeth. What to do?

What had happened?

The sound of the motors faded away. He felt that it was going to rain. North wind. But he was determined to learn. He had already asked a lot of people in the street. Everybody pretended they didn't hear him or that they didn't know. As though they had broken off all connections with that mythical time before the bombs, leaving them only with that black umbilicus, an open, toothless, wordless mouth. Everyone had lost something in the bombardment. A left arm. A foot. A couple of ears. A few eyes, but not many.

He was determined to find out why he couldn't live without his pacifier.

They were telling him that he was too old now. But times were hard, the unexpected was the order of the day, role models difficult to find. He liked the taste of rubber in his mouth. Won't it give you cancer, his mother said to him one time while she was dusting the desk. Although she wasn't exactly happy about the increasing drug store bill. His teeth were very sharp. Children his age used to laugh at him. But then his tremendous talent for soccer manifested itself, giving promise of reaching legendary proportions in his neighborhood before long. A great passer, great dribbler, great goal kicker, great goalie. What would he be best at? He scratched the scars on his face. He was grateful that they kept drying up. But he mustn't scratch. They were getting better but hadn't disappeared. It was a tremendous temptation nevertheless. It was so easy to scratch oneself. Without thinking. Yawning. On one leg. Without talking. Sucking on the pacifier. Sharp nails. To stop the itching. But he had to bear it. If he could only catch the pesky fly that buzzed around the end of his nose. He loved to watch them struggling to rise and slip back and fall and try again and fall again and the horror they must feel on discovering that they no longer had wings.

What had happened?

He came down from the roof. The fly was annoying him. The sun suddenly went down. If his nostrils swelled he had to stuff Vicks into them. His mother would soon be calling him for another lesson. He preferred to go out and kick the ball around. His faithful gang loping towards the crazies' park. His toes itching to make contact with the leather.

How many did that make, now? New elections were called. It would have been his second year in school. The number of candidates was held down to forty. A committee headed by the Archbishop was appointed to assess their moral attributes. It was required that they know the Pater Noster by heart in Latin and some of the candidates objected. The

Spanish version was enough, they claimed. Latin was a dead language. And the interim government began to fear a new uprising. But no. Sanity prevailed. Those who protested were picked up and put before the firing squad. The government gave their widows a pension. The number of applicants decreased.

A certain amount of tension was beginning to be felt, brows furrowed, light dimmed. There was disagreement. Horrors! A disagreement? Disagreement. Who would be the civilian candidate to lose the election? In all due respect for the people, a civilian candidate was always a necessity. The generals were the ones who couldn't agree. Each had his favorite fool. But they wanted one who would, of course, be smart enough to win the confidence of the public. Patience came to an end. There was no trusting science. A state of siege with a liberal midnight curfew was declared. Common sense won out. The disagreement was cleared up. An agreement was reached.

Each general put forward his favorite's name. An elimination contest was arranged to be held probably in the National Stadium, the country's health and fitness mecca, with all profits to go into the fund for a new Officers' Club. The grand winner would have the patriotic honor of seeing his name on the losing slate in the upcoming free and democratic election. The U.S. Ambassador promised to purchase a block of seats for himself, family, employees, and assistants.

The contest was a great success. A Finnish architect was brought in to design a new Officers' Club made entirely of glass in the form of an officers' cap. Many jobs were created. The liquor industry opened two new distilleries.

The whores came out from the very beginning in favor of General Idigyorass's candidate. After the first two elimination rounds the people began to catch on. Rumors flew from house to house. Everybody thought the prosties knew something they didn't. A few cries of fraud were heard but so few and so faint that they weren't worth bothering about. The whores must have already seen him in action and been aware of his strong and weak points, that inimitable style of his. They were, of course, always in a position to know such things. The populace learned to put their money where the providential prostitutes did.

On a bright and cheery day in June, when Máximo would have been taking his midterms, had classes not been suspended so that all the nation's school children might go to the stadium to be enlightened by the grand finale. The prices, astronomical. But that didn't matter. Nothing mattered. One of the small sacrifices history demands of people in exchange for their beloved, believed-in, and besought democracy. The stadium had been sold out for months. If one was not lucky enough to be a ticket holder, there was only one recourse. The black market. And the blowing of one's life savings to attend the latest, greatest, mostest of all spectacles. The contest of contests, standoff of standoffs. Titan vs. titan, win or lose. Fully aware of the interest that had built up over the event and considering the stadium's seating capacity of 100,001, the acting president gave his personal assurance, a guarantee sealed with blood and fire, that this time the Gillette Sports Cavalcade would carry the broadcast tremor by tremor, gasp by gasp, to the very heart of each and every home in the nation. *Eveready* was ready to cover the expenses and a world-class figure in the world of sports came to the country to give his world-class comments on the sensational event.

The bright and cheery day in June arrived soaked. What had started out around midnight as a slight drizzle became a storm of major proportions within a few hours. Lighting was still flashing across the vault of the sky at dawn and the sound of thunder boomed like Indian drums with rivers of water pouring furiously along all the streets, the tremendous volume of water carrying away the humble possessions of the overburdened sewers. With tears in their eyes the generals were obliged to postpone the event.

It was rescheduled for the following Sunday but that day came and the rain had not stopped. General Idigyorass hurried to confession. And it kept raining. The world-class figure of the sports world left for Sumatra to be the commentator at an international diplomatic ping-pong tournament. And it kept raining. The prices on the black market began to drop. And it kept raining. And it kept raining. And it kept raining and raining and raining.

One day in mid-July at four in the afternoon or so, a carter on his way from Chinautla with a load of beautiful Chinautla pottery, Pokomán culture, pulverized clay, hand-modeled, decoration of the same clay, sand-bed fired, etc., said that he had seen the sun peeping from behind an angry purple crab-shaped cloud. Rainbows began to appear soon after.

One was seen to the south of the city over the two mountains that guard the entrance to the Amatitlán valley. Another was reported toward the Northeast, behind Cows Bridge in the general direction of Xaxón. Some people were saying that there was another one behind the parade grounds to the Southeast. There was a rainbow in the mountains and in the city. Rainbows could be seen downtown, children pointing at them. Rainbows could be seen from the little farms in the ravines where the tortilla makers tried to ignore them. Umbrellas began closing in the downtown streets. A flock of larks planed toward the main square and flew in formation over the Avenue of Freedom flooding the whole area with their song. General Idigyorass ran to the Carmelite church to kiss the feet of the Virgin of the Forty Little Eyes. He sent for his colleagues. Soldiers went to every corner of the city announcing that the great event would take place the next day, a Saturday, at 4.00 p.m. The young pluviologist brought all the way from Cherrapunji, India by the U.S. Ambassador despite his Brahman lover's distress, extracted a promise that he would be paid his full fee even if nature won the race. The witch doctors were let out of jail after they signed a document promising not to light any magic bonfires for a period of no less than 72 hours. It was read to them before they were forced to put their mark on the page. The price of tickets began to go up.

Rah, rah, rah, sis boom bah, alaveevo, alavaivo, alaveevo, vaivo, voo! The Kid, The Kid, we want you!

At seven in the morning the lines were already interminable. Thermos bottles and lunch boxes stretched for blocks and blocks from the Avenue of Athletes, under the railroad bridge, passing through the Alley of the Lame, The Avenue of Misfortune, the Boulevard of Hairy-Chested Machos, the Alley of the Dispossessed, Ground Corn Square, and Cat Piss Lane, as far as Station Avenue, climbing to Barrios Square, and ending at the Calvary Church steps where the acolytes were selling incense and *tostadas* with beans. Shifty characters hung around the gates offering fistfuls of bills for a ticket. Peddlers running up and down the the long lines hawking oranges, oranges with salt and chili, fruit drinks of all flavors, pineapple and tamarind, sweet rolls, sacks of potato chips, peanuts at 5 centavos a bag, salted popcorn. Bottles were not allowed into the stadium for fear that some overwrought fan might throw one at the field and seriously injure a presidential candidate. Everybody was frisked before entering. Everybody was buying sun shades because of the glare. Red ones, and green and blue, too, lots of sun shades, and some wore palm leaf hats and dark glasses. Policemen and soldiers with machine guns in evidence everywhere, guardians of order, smiling, to ensure the peaceful course of the event. Curious vultures perched on the crests of the cypress trees around the stadium. It was a festive occasion.

Rah, rah, rah, sis boom bah, alaveevo, alavaivo, alaveevo vaivo, voo! The Kid, The Kid, We want you!

A roaring mass of humanity already there by noontime. Shouts, obscenities cutting through the air, sodas spilt on unwitting victims, lost children, men fighting, couples quarreling. But only one woman smothered to death. Shouts of the cheering squads in the south stands. Rah, rah, rah, sis boom bah! Confetti flying, of all colors, blood red, motherland blue, hope purple, and shit green. In the north stands two overheated men, alcohol, rolling on top of surprised spectators after having referred to their respective mothers in disrespectful terms. An oily-haired woman in a tattered jacket egging them on. Things calmed down with the sound of shots, a wonderful elixir of peace in heaven and on earth, in the city and the mountains.

The Kid! The Kid! The Kid!

The national anthem. Everybody stood. An endless line of fat generals and pink-cheeked men in top hats began taking their places in the section reserved for guests of honor. The acting president, somebody said, pointing at a short little man who walked with an ivory cane. Behind him, General Idigyorass. It was said that he had a glass eye. General Peralta Absurdo. General Arriando Bosque. General "Spider" Arana. General Shell Genial Longitud. The spectators began to yawn.

After some five minutes the two finalists entered the stadium through the Triumphal Arch, standing over it the inspired statue of the disheveled angel, a present to General Carrera from Napoleon III. The spectators on their feet, jumping up and down, yelling, rockets bursting, eyes wet with tears, arms waving, confetti, more confetti, bright colors everywhere, insignias, two bands playing different selections. Several fans trying to jump the barrier to shake hands with their heroes. Some women fainted but not many. Children waved flags energetically and five people danced on the stairs, newspapers were set on fire, torches in the air, bonfires on the steps, the smoke starting to rise.

The Kid! The Kid! The Kid!

General Idigyorass' man was Cayetano Fuentes. Shockingly tall and stout as an old ceiba tree, a manly man without a doubt but with a surprisingly high voice, a characteristic, some suggested, that cast doubt on certain aspects of his nature, giving rise to his nickname, "The Maybe Kid." Others thought maybe otherwise. Chicanery in the entrance exams was rumored. The candidates were assumed to know how to read and write. But there had been enough delay, the top officials said, in refusing to investigate. They had no more time to waste. The country was ready for, the country needed, democracy. The Inter-American Development Bank insisted on elections. There was no stipulation in any known document in the world that required a candidate to be able to read and write. The chairman of the Fruit Company had said in a now quite famous interview that, personally, he preferred candidates who couldn't. Why waste any more time on aspersions cast by sore losers, malcontents, enemies of progress and order, why pay attention to Communists, atheists, intellectuals, social parasites? The people were for The Maybe Kid. The people were the law as in any true democracy, any government of the people, by the people, for the people, in spite of the people. A new group of technical advisers bearing gifts was seen arriving at the airport.

Rah, rah, rah, sis boom bah. Alaveevo, alavaivo, alaveevo, vaivo, voo. The Kid, The Kid, The Kid, We want you!

There was a wooden dais in the center of the stadium field. Completely covered by the flag. Behind, the metal chairs occupied by the band. On the dais, the table. Rectangular, varnished and highly polished, with four chairs, one on each side. Two for the judges, gentlemen of unimpeachable rectitude, ever ready to obey their officers. General Idigyorass, leaning back in his seat, drumming with his fingers on his swelling paunch. He took out a toothpick which he poked between his gleaming teeth. The rumored glass eye contemplating the task of governing a well-behaved, well-educated society. The judges drew two large Xs with chalk on the combat table and lit the candles. A roar from the crowd.

Elbows on the Xs. Hands touched, gripped, felt the other's sweat, the taut throbbing thumbs. Arms bare to the shoulder, every muscle clearly outlined. Tense. Quivering. Anticipating the bursts of energy. The trumpeter stood up, eyes fixed on the reviewing stand where the U.S. Ambassador, almost ill at ease, and completely without expression, raised his hat. A blast from the trumpet hit the air, shouts from the expectant crowd, the silence that followed, the judges in their places, the thundering of the drums. Go!

Contraction of muscles. Bones creaking. Drops of sweat appearing, faces empurpled. Teeth grating, giving out sparks. Saliva trickling from compressed lips in foamy waves. Flat noses expanding, spreading toward their ears. Eyes nearly shut, a blue-black line like a knife edge. the public engrossed in the show, hypnotized. The candle flames dancing to the caresses of the wind.

Locked. Neither giving. Quivering. Shaking. Shaking violently, as though in a common epileptic fit. Arms like steel, steel towers. Turning red, purple, turning black with the passing of eternal seconds, glistening, silvered in the sunlight. A judge staring in fascination at the droplets of blood trickling from the elbow that was sinking into the wood like an augur bit. A long interval of silence broken only by a sudden sigh, a slight sob, the clumping of a tensed muscle. As though asleep in their position, petrified, a statue, thousands of pairs of eyes upon those swelling, sweating towers. And then a new surge of energy. Both men jumping spasmodically as one, trying to overpower the other, rattling the table with a crescendo of exploding muscles, one against another, upon tendon and bone. The strain greater, more desperate. Gigantic white fingers calling for the prodigious effort, to crush the life out of the other's fingers, to put an end to the pain. Neither yielding a millimeter. The fingers, white and black, as the pressure mounted or waned, hearts bursting, leaping out of their breasts. A judge raised his eyes. Saw the hungry incisors burying themselves in the flesh of the lower lip. Blood all around, everywhere. The thirsty tongue, a huge tired ox, sliding slowly, stickily, seeking the precious fluid, to stave off thirst. Both as though immersed in an immense tank of water, drowning. The eyes of one so tightly closed that they disappeared completely. Solemnly listening to his pounding heart. Appeased, dulled, the burning rain of sweat from the eyebrows, from between the eyebrows, from the lips, running from the cheeks, dripping from the end of the nose. The nausea of the sound of the spectators, the mass of colors, vaguely sensed in the distance. The noise. Far away. Everything going round and round senselessly, formlessly, expressionlessly. Their arms the center of the world.

And suddenly the wave of muscles no longer responding. Tendons melting down, escaping control, pain. All over with. Flash of light in the right temple, fogged vision, broken connection, realization, acceptance, intense pain boring through the arm, unconscious pain, burning the nerves, the senses.

Head fallen to the center of the table. One of the judges shouted and jumped to push the hand over the flame of the judgement candle, nauseated by the smell of burnt skin. The opponent seated, impassive, contemplating the loser, uncomprehending. A long silence, agonizing, mercifully broken by the burst of applause. The band rose to play.

General Idigyorass jumped up and down in his seat like a little boy. Hoarse, he hastened to open the box of cigars and offered the first to the U.S. Ambassador who smiled politely. An assistant at his ear: the French Ambassador was also a smoker. But with that deafening noise, that noise. The people dancing in the stands. Just as they had been instructed to. Some sang and applauded. Just as they had been instructed to. The band marched around the stadium as the crowd deliriously waved their flags. Just as they had been instructed to. Beautiful women stripping off their clothes and trying to leap over the barrier to offer themselves at the victor's feet. Just as they had been instructed to. Warning shots in the air that nobody could hear anymore. The light-hearted Archbishop squeezed his sexton's hand. The vultures pirouetted in the sky.

Well, that's how we are, son, just a lot of noise. Always having a ball, and to mariachi music. It boils up your blood but leaves you with nothing but a gummy hangover. And as your father used to say, what the hell!

Máximo was walking down the street. It was only two blocks to the crazies' park. He spotted an empty can in the middle of the the street. He kicked it hard trying to score in the mouth of a sewer. Missed by inches. The can hit the edge of the sidewalk and bounced the entire length of the street.

And will I ever be going to school? I don't know. It's up to them.

Maybe his whole school career would consist of sitting out suspended classes and changes in government. He asked his mother, always asked her, and she always answered that it wouldn't surprise her, nothing would surprise her, turning around to passionately inhale the smell of burnt food stuck to the bottom of the pot.

What would the school buildings be like?

Smaller than a stadium without a doubt and lots more windows to throw stones at. With a lady teacher in the middle of the classroom giving an arithmetic lesson and threatening to shoot the pupil in the last row who had just spit on the floor.

But he didn't need school. He wanted to be a soccer player and for that you couldn't beat the streets. Or could you? Because he wanted to be a soccer player, and if he wanted to be a soccer player then be a soccer player, said his mother, as she sat by the window sticking her tongue out at the ladies in black hurrying to six o'clock mass. Being a soccer player was all that one could aspire to these days, she said to him, the only thing these days, not to be compared to those gone by, before your father, before.

Tell me more, tell me more, tell me more. But she said no more, nothing that he didn't already know. Yes, it had been before the bombs. Everything had been before the bombs, always before the bombs. When there were schools, and milk, and dreams. But where is he now? Where is he? And she threatened to hit him with the fly swatter if he didn't shut up. He ran to the street, she pulling her hair and screaming at him that the mosquitoes would come and eat him up if he didn't stop asking.

Who had brought those horrible bombs that had made his father go away?

He crossed the street and found another can to kick. He aimed carefully but missed again. And then he heard shouting in the next street.

Could it be the revolution?

Because he didn't know what a revolution was but he did know that revolutions sometimes marched in the street in very beautiful parades with bands and carriages and beautiful cheerleaders shouting things that rhymed. Pacha, his skinny friend with the big mole over his right eyebrow, said that one day he had followed a revolution along the Street of Visions. A rainy afternoon, he said it was, and he followed it until it disappeared at an uncertain corner. He had no money to buy a souvenir but his mother told him they were all made in Japan. His friend was a good goalie.

Máximo saw the group of soldiers dragging the man towards the park. He ran, wanting to catch up with them, to see. They were dragging him by the hair, by the arms, and his shirt was torn, his pants. When one of them would hit him in the back with his rifle butt the others laughed. One of the soldiers had a bunch of papers in his hand and was carrying some of those square things his mother called books. He had heard of them. Bigger boys had told him stuff.

The man falling down all the time, taking such a long time to get to the park, Máximo bored and wanting to play but his friends not there yet. There was a big ceiba tree in the middle of the park that cast a tremendous shadow. Yawning, he leaned against the trunk to watch the soldiers.

He wondered where the crazy people were. At that time of day they could usually be seen doing calisthenics all in a single line. They would march in different formations. They played games with make-believe balls. They would laugh a lot and for a long time and didn't shave. Máximo loved to watch them. Too bad, he liked them so much, too bad they weren't there.

The soldiers dropped the books and papers into a hole. A big hole it must have been, they all fitted in so good, so easy. The man got away from them and jumped on top of the pile of books and papers. They pulled him out by the feet. He hugged the books, clutching on to them. And they began to beat him with hoses. Máximo saw a soldier lifting his head up by the hair and hitting him in the face, in the face, hitting him, hitting him in the face.

He could feel the pain.

Máximo covered his face. He was feeling it, was seeing it. He stroked his still tender scars and bit his pacifier, feeling it, and hearing the long-drawn-out groan. He looked up. Saw the bonfire.

Máximo ran towards the bonfire. A soldier jumped in his way.

What are you doing?

We're burning the Devil.

Those papers?

They're *his* papers.

And what are you burning them for?

He's a Communist.

He studied the leaping flames, licking at each other, stroking each other's backs, first one, then another, growing bigger and stronger with each devoured page, blackening, breaking apart and disappearing with the fatal caresses, lost, folding inwards, exposing their sides, their last cries of pain silenced in the momentary dance, until not a single word was left. Máximo recalled that he didn't care about books.

What's a Communist?

The soldiers looked at him, at each other, looked at him again. One of them brought the hose to his chest pressing it against himself with the open palm of the other hand, like a shield. Máximo recognized the surprise in his smile.

Don't any of you know?

One soldier was kneeling on the man's back. The man alone, stretched out on the ground, his pupils dancing in rhythm with the last of the flames, the blood from his gashed lips coursing liberally down his chin, dripping onto the grass. In the distance, he could hazily make out a Chinese magician threading needles with his mouth while standing on one leg.

It was superstitious material.

Subversive, man, don't be a horse's ass.

Okay, subversive? The same shit.

Máximo watching the man who was staring at him, at him, and Máximo kept on and the man, his wild expression just like the crazy people, his crazy people whose absence he'd been regretting just a few minutes before. And, yes, it was also the look of the old man who had told him his first story, the old man who was going no place, in his eyes, all of them the same.

He writes against our government, our morals, and our church.

And the man began to laugh, a thin, uncertain little laugh that opened, expanded, and the man said, lies, kid, I write for you, he was saying, laughing, and crying, all at the same time, tears running down his mud-covered cheeks. The soldiers not knowing what to do, hesitating, not understanding, he's crazy, he's crazy, isn't he? He's crazy? Máximo nodding his head, he's crazy, of course, how could he not be, he liked the crazy people so much, where were the crazy people today, the others? The last of the books was now burning.

I am in the kingdom of words and what frightens them is the truth that words reflect in their silence. What? That words can express what everybody prefers not to say. People who prefer silence, lies, conformity.

Máximo saw the soldier smash the rifle butt into his kidneys. His body arched and his head stretched forward seeking to bite the air, yellowed teeth, burying themselves now in the grass in a vomit of blood and bile.

Take him away. He's won himself a scholarship to Panama.

The soldier pulled him by the legs, dragging his body through the mud, the inert head bouncing on the stones, skin torn by dark glass shards. Máximo's eyes fixed on the puddle of vomit that reflected the soldiers against the sky. Each little clump of grass folding under his weight. Little sticks covered over, too. There was red on the lumps of mud. Red. Red and mud. He looked at the man who was a distance away. All those bodies. All those bodies. Yes, strewn on the streets. The bombs. After the bombs. Countless puddles of blood that he had jumped over without thinking anything more than that his feet might get wet. Blinded by the rain he had kicked bodies. The old man had told him a story and disappeared. And it had been hailing. Times must have been different before the bombs, had to be. When people like his father helped do things. The soldiers were drawing out of sight. The body covered with mud. A new wound in his forehead pouring blood. His back and chest almost bare. When people like his father, oh, people like his father. He ran after them, reached them, pushed close to the man, excited, agitated.

Do they do this to everyone?

The soldiers standing, hesitating. Máximo saw the man trying to open his swollen eye.

Sentimentality is as boring as talking about the weather. Perversity is where it's at.

But one soldier raised his rifle and pointed it at Máximo, aimed it at his head. He almost swallowed his pacifier, but politely pushing the barrel aside, mumbling excuse me, he knelt beside the man.

Where's my father? Where can I find him?

Your father? You have a father? You're looking for your father? A father?

Yes.

Look in the ashes of my books.

The soldier picked Máximo up by the waist and threw him like a ball. He fell on top of some dry leaves, they rustled, he felt his head bounce against the ground, hard, damp, his hips absorbing the pain. He stayed there without moving, tasting the earth, salty, letting the pain climb up his spine, sliding in behind his head, taking it all up.

That crazy man was good-looking, he thought, but he couldn't talk. Colors disappear the same way.

When he got to his feet there wasn't a trace of the soldiers or the man. He looked and all he could see was the Chinese magician threading needles with his mouth while standing on one leg. The crazy people had been let out, they were already there, happily watching the magic show, sitting on their make-believe chairs. He could hear the applause.

Every bone, every muscle hurt. He brushed off his trousers, his hands, and wished it would rain as he approached the ashes of the bonfire.

The wind was blowing away flakes of ash. They floated. And he could see the remains, the binding of one of the books. Light brown, one golden letter going nowhere. He squatted, sank his hands into the ashes. They were still warm. The kingdom of words. He pulled his hands out, lifted them. Ashes everywhere, scattering, carried by the wind into every corner, the words. Enough to cover the park, to block up the sewers and gutters. And the crazy people were walking along the side of the park in single file beating their fists against their foreheads. He got so close to the ashes that the tip of his nose was all gray.

I'll find you, father.

He wiped his mouth with his bare arm and walked slowly away.

When the great contest was over, The Maybe Kid was officially declared the civilian candidate, new elections were called for the end of the year. The Maybe Kid was popular and covered the country from end to end, his right arm in a sling, urging all decent folks to vote for General Idigyorass. The people listened in bewilderment and the Archbishop predicted that a series of plagues, yes, consider yourselves on notice, plagues, would be visited on the homes of all renegades who did not heed the word of God. God, it was said confidentially, already had plans for new investments to develop the country.

On a bright and cheery Sunday in December, the people came out to vote. The Archbishop was in the main square selling balloons to the children for five centavos while their parents were being told for whom to vote. A soldier with a machine gun stood at each ballot box as a visual reminder to conscientious citizens. The people were all smiles.

And the welcome news on the front pages the next day. General Idigyorass by absolute majority, with a photograph of the surprised winner kissing his proud wife slightly uneasy at the thought of the enormous responsibility suddenly to be hers as First Lady. His first official proclamation was that the coming year was to be a year of national celebration. Democracy had returned to the Republic. It was every citizen's duty to celebrate the vindication of common sense. There was order for the first time since the bombings.

Máximo was surprised to see so much broken glass in the street. It glittered more brightly than ever in the afternoon sun. There was order, he repeated, yes, remembering the writer.

He crossed the street and saw his friends already playing. Rodri, Rodri racing, Rodri dribbling, Rodri waiting, with his heavy legs, Rodri, so squat but so fast on his feet, dribbling through two of the defense, leaving them behind, swerving to the left, arching his body, and the cannonball as deep as it could go. But Pacha. Pacha the goalie. Pacha waiting, leaping in the air, deflecting the ball at the last instant. Shouts, arm upraised. Rodri frustrated, kicking dirt, raising a cloud of dust, the dirty swearword, trotting gracefully for the corner. The area in front of the goal a mass of black mud. Máximo instinctively heading for his position ready to play. But he stopped. He looked at them. The corner kick came in high, all jumped. Rodri, the shortest, Rodri beating them all to the jump, nudging the ball with his forehead, the powerful neck tendons, towards the goal posts. There could be no greater pleasure than getting into a game, Máximo had no doubt of that.

He bit his pacifier and backed up.

So many doubts, emotions, reactions. So many. What did those soldiers mean? What was a scholarship to Panama? Panama. He had to know. To make his mother talk. And he wanted to know about words, yes, about words.

Goal? The yell hanging in the air, more a howl than a shout. Goal? He turned around. Rodri and his teammates hugging one another, slaps on the back, returning to the center of the field at a trot. Pacha prone in the mud. A desolate figure chasing after the treacherous ball in the distance. Maybe if he waited. A day or two wouldn't change anything, right? He had a whole lifetime to learn about words. Why bother his mother? She had a headache that afternoon. What the devil, why not? He wiped the sweat from his hands on the back of his trousers.

Hey, guys, I'm coming in!

CHAPTER 4

FIRST LOVE

What do you mean you can't work if the bed isn't made? The dust doesn't seem to bother you. All you do is watch TV, the goddam TV. Why...

But he was talking to the air. She'd already switched him off. She was gone, off someplace else... Actually, he couldn't have cared less.

Go get me another banana.

He looked at her. Yes, he did think she was a beauty. Not pretty pretty. Beautiful that came on strong. Everything so modernistic, though, who could stand it. The desk. A plain glass box. Who ever heard of a transparent desk? And all those mirrors on the wall. Too many reflections for his taste. Brilliance that also came on strong. He preferred darkness to this brightness, so bright it could drive one crazier than the darkness he was used to. She, naked. Her eyes glued to the TV. And the long milky fingers automatically stroking that long silky hair. Tow-head. Like the sun, like the sun but not quite white.

How about the banana, okay?

He left the room and came back with the required piece of fruit.

Can I tell you a dream I had?

I'd rather listen to music, she said. And dance the twist, twist, twist! But you said just before that you wanted to hear it, that was what you told me. But that was before. And couldn't he be more considerate? He was leaning against the antenna. He moved. He was sure there was a misunderstanding. He would like to tell her that. That his interest had its limits. He liked her small breasts. But she was so exasperating. He respected her virginity. He liked being with her, and looking at her, and talking to her sometimes, when she wasn't so full of crap. Now she had eaten half the banana and with her free hand was undoing little tangles in her scanty pubic hairs.

Come on. Let's take a walk. In the crazies' park. Or in Las Conchas.

But no. She preferred the goddam television. No wind or cold with TV, no need to get dressed, people only a dream, the noise under control. A small button on the right above the vertical, horizontal, and brilliance controls. The creation of the world itself. Why venture into something you can't control? Anyway, the streets in the city are nothing but bricks with holes in them.

He threatened to tell her his dreams. If you do it with a slide show, she said, winking, in the knowledge that words alone weren't enough. He shrugged, didn't care, and went for the projector. Old slides her father had taken when he was first here. She threw the banana peel in the middle of the floor.

On the wall a faint image of a volcano, upside down. She cackled.

The Agua Volcano, Karen.

I know, stupid.

It's the most beautiful volcano in the world. Don't let the Japanese tell you any different.

And she seeing it in her mind's eye with the crown of stars around the crater: Paramount Pictures. Delicious memories of long, endless nights stretched out in front of her little Sony.

It flooded the capital in 1541, Karen. Drowned Doña Ventura sin Cueva, the wife of the conquistador whom the Indians called Tonadiú because he was as blond as you.

She yawned. If you must bore me, tell me about revolutions and that kind of crap. Something to make John Wayne's eyes sparkle, Charlton Heston's upper lip tremble. He turned off the projector. And now what's with you? She lay down full length on the carpet like a cat. Oh, Max. She gave him a couple of pats on the calf. I get bored quickly. She didn't have the energy to withdraw her hand. And anyway what do I care about your dreams. Tropical crap. I admit that little hill is prettier than Westport, Connecticut. He sat on top of her and began tickling her. Seriously, Max. Dreams should be killed.

What was Westport like? He had never been there. Never been out of the country. A rich people's town on Long Island Sound, she always called it. What the fuck was a Long Island sound? He always wanted to ask her. But she was already watching television, picking her nose.

I had an allergy when I was a little kid, Karen. See these scars. It's the lack of warmth that makes my face heal so slowly.

She turned the volume all the way down, leaving the picture on.

Just talking crap. Thinking too much causes asthma, Max. Look at us. We never think. All we do is watch television and we're masters of three-quarters of the world. Why can't you be like us?

Her wink drew a smile from him. And she went back to her beloved Sony...with *Efrem Zimabalist, Jr.* He watched her. *Presented to you by...* She had forgotten he was there. *Tonight's episode...* He remembered that she wanted to climb a volcano in eruption.

Her name, so hard for Máximo to say, was Karen Johnson, and was she his first love or not? Her father, the president of the Monsanto branch in the country and taking over as acting ambassador. The ambassador had been called to Washington right after the tragic fall of General Idigyorass who had had to leave the country, his nose swollen. Máximo thought that her height might be the key factor. She was six inches taller than he.

But at least she spoke Spanish.

And the year had started out with a new government but General Peralta Absurdo had a face like a cauliflower and the people did not have much confidence in him. The disruption caused by old Idigyorass's swelling had brought on the inevitable state of siege and closing of the schools. But, of course, the government gave everybody credit for the year and now Máximo was getting ready to enter junior high school.

Would he ever attend a school?

His mother, battier than ever, in a new fit of fury, had climbed on a third-class bus to the coast where she was going to cultivate the sublime. She sat in a chair every morning facing the sea, swaying with a dozen other women.

He liked Karen because she could twist that false ear of hers around like the dial on a radio.

But now she had dozed off on him, the sleeping beauty of his dreams, and there was nothing to be done about it. He picked up his windbreaker, closed the door silently, and headed down the street.

It was only eight o'clock. Three hours to kill before curfew. What to do. Pacha telling him that tonight with Rodri at The Last Goodbye, a cantina opposite the cemetery. To The Last Goodbye, then. He pulled the pacifier out of his breast pocket, its rubbery odor tickling his nostrils before he put it carefully over his tongue. There were so few stars in the sky.

With love and strong drink, why bother to think, tra la la.

Unable to concentrate, Karen and volcanoes. He had a nice pair of holes in the soles of his shoes. His toenails blessing the fresh air. Just then a bicycle went by.

Hey, your light's out.

The rider gave a start, looked at him, leaned forward to check, all the way over, lost his balance, wobbled from side to side, knees up in the air before turning all the way around, bicycle and all, plunging headfirst, the bicycle on top of him. He ran to help him.

I'm sorry.

He helped the man up, to brush the dust off his long wrinkled coat, a big hooked nose, potbellied. Dressed in very old clothes, practically no soles left on his shoes. If he had had a beard he'd have been an appealing figure.

Don't worry about it. The eternal dream of the man of action is to rediscover the primitive security of the instincts in an infinitely more complex form.

Inspecting his vehicle carefully, lovingly.

Where were you going?

I wasn't going. I was returning some books to the library. I was learning about the transference of thought and instinct.

Well, I'm getting together with a couple of buddies and having some drinks. Want to join us?

I mustn't put the blame on these books but I have to get rid of them first. Sad but true, they're long overdue.

I'll keep you company. May I have a look at them?

The man handed over the books. *Being and Time. The ABC of Relativity. Homo Ludens. The Quest for Identity.* They were heavy volumes and the golden letters on the red bindings reflected the street light. He opened *The Quest for Identity.* The man smiled. What a surprise! The pages were blank. He opened the others. Blank, also.

But they're blank.

Obviously. By any chance are there methods that enable man to direct his thoughts in such a way that his resulting actions will find an easy path between beings and things?

I'm afraid not...

Their contents are illegal, young man, illegal under the law. A person can be shot for possessing the contents of any book printed in this century. With the possible exception of the Boy Scout Handbook.

But you were reading them!

To advance my knowledge. There were certain doubts to be cleared up, concepts to be expanded. Otherwise, I'm not able to believe, not able to do.

But how can you read them if they're blank?

With my imagination. It is not reason that tells the sculptor to steepen the curve of the hip...

I'm lost in your words.

They walked. Máximo with Karen's pointy little breasts inside his head. Frightened by the deathly whiteness of the books. Books, already beginning to pursue him. He stepped on some broken glass that groaned stridently, frightening off a couple of rats that were rooting in the garbage. And such fantasies about his disappeared father. Both of them, to pass time, whispering songs to themselves. The same song, they discovered.

> I'm back now from where I was
> They allowed me to return.
> And me never figuring
> I'd ever see you again.

A quick stop at the library and on to the cantina. The man with the bicycle over his shoulder looked so normal, his gaze lost in the distance. Those eyes. Máximo wanted to talk, to question, his mind a crossroads of ideas, but nothing came out, he didn't dare, everything so blurry. Pairs of little eyes, so many pairs of little eyes, appearing and disappearing in the darkness. He kicked an empty can. The noise and all the little eyes disappeared.

My girlfriend wants to climb a volcano in eruption.

Really? Might she not be one herself? A fire dies down if not fed, you should know. Love must be continually fortified. Good exercise for the thighs.

Walking along. He was beginning to find himself walking all the time. Small swarms of moths blocking out the street lights. An army jeep passed and the two instinctively tensed. They could hear the soldier's taunting laugh. His companion wiped his mouth with his hand, so yellow, shaking.

I like books. I once saw a whole bonfire of books.

You should take her to Pacaya. Fuego Volcano is too dangerous. But warn her not to wear high heels. Love is fickle but no doubt you can squeeze certain concessions out of it.

Those pointy breasts, bowing politely to greet him. More attractive from far away, the farther away from her the better. He wasn't even noticing the wind.

But my passion has always been soccer.

I seek meaning, an explanation. I see a thousand motivations in every factor of my life.

Parrots are my favorite birds.

Occasionally I like to be trembling all the time. Muscles working against muscles. Like musical notes in half-filled bottles.

I've been going to The Last Goodbye with Pacha and Rodri since I was twelve years old. Even though I'm still allergic to hard liquor.

What happens to the Jungian when he dies? Where does he go? I wonder.

But I'm scared of dogs. Especially German shepherds.

Religion coalesces the collective stupidity of our race. Just look at the little Spaniard who passes himself off as our Archbishop. But it's against the law for him to be a native. The top authorities are afraid that he will identify with his countrymen. The Fruit Company picks ambassadors the same way.

And then I saw that poor writer being dragged away. He was bleeding from the nose.

I'd like to invite Heidegger to do a rain dance. He'd put the local witch doctors to shame.

My mother began to cry, then she hugged me and promised to tell me more about my father. But when I asked her again she burned the beans.

Syntactic links have to be broken.

What?

What about what?

About what you were saying.

What I was saying about what?

Being broken.

Yes, that.

What?

What about it?

What you were saying about it?

What I was saying?

Yes, that.

What?

That you broke it without tactics.

Oh. Merely a declaration of intention. I haven't gotten around to doing it yet.

You talk funny.

My nose's fault. Pay me no mind.

It's bigger. Tell me. Are books a way of passing the time between lovers or are lovers a way of passing the time between books?

Would you like to sleep with your books?

You'll like my friends. What's your name?

Chingolo.

Sounds like Pocholo. I had a teddy bear named Pocholo but my mother tore him up the day Batista fell.

Revolutions tend to be circular in nature and disrespectful of time. But that type of victim is generally an exception the size of China.

It was New Year's Eve and I'd been to the movies. I think it was the twenty-sixth time I tried to see The Big Circus with Cliff Robertson and Esther Williams but the line was still seven blocks long. It had been like that since July. I prowled around for a couple of hours before giving up and going off to the crazies' park to watch them exercising and asking myself as usual why they didn't shave. My friends weren't there. But there were ice-cream vendors everywhere. I wanted an ice cream like anything but didn't remember that I had money in my pocket. One of the crazy people was laughing at me in my predicament and jumping up and down, waving his arms. When I finally began to laugh too, he got excited, encouraging me to keep up with him, yes, keep it up, more and more, laughing, mouth wide open, until he was roaring with laughter, doubled over, holding his stomach, tears streaming from his eyes. And then he served me a huge helping of make-believe ice cream. It was delicious. Pistachio and French Vanilla with nuts and a very red, round maraschino cherry on top. I was enjoying it for a long time before I went home. It was starting to get dark. I took my time, kicking every little stone on my way. I'm specially good at scoring on the half-turn. With the left foot, like Culiche. A difficult kick, I'd say. And it was dark when I got home. The radios were all going full blast in the neighborhood, talk, talk, like a soccer game broadcast, you know what I mean, when the announcers are going out of their minds and begin yelling that Culiche steals the ball, passes to Boots Martínez, Martínez to Pericullo coming up from behind, stopping dead, dodging Tin Tan, faking, then lofting the ball to meet Pinulita racing over to break to his right, leaving Geronazzo hanging, and he gets loose, advances, dribbling once, twice, the center coming up, Vetorazzi stretching elegantly, the ball getting away from him as Pensamiento comes in and heads the ball, and gooaall! But I knew there was no game scheduled and figured it must be a new state of siege and let it go at that until I realized it couldn't be, everybody in such high spirits, and on a night like this, what general would dare on New Year's Eve? The commentators interrupting each other, saying one thing, and another, voices cracking, hoarse, squeaking. Latest flash. It had to be something political, they never give news flashes unless it's political, flash always meaning something's going on, flash, somebody got killed, flash, somebody tried a takeover, flash, somebody got dumped. Flash, flash, flash until I got home. I saw my mother dancing in the living room, holding her long skirt up with her two hands as if she was doing a cancan, shaking the ends of her skirt, bending at the waist in all directions, kicking up her legs in front and then in back, an idiotic smile on her face. She had news of my father was my first thought, seeing her there with stockings rolled up over the knee and singing hoarse and out of tune. The whole house smelled of liquor and me yelling, mother, what happened, mother? She ran over to hug me and give me a kiss on the forehead, the radios going at full blast, kissing me without leaving off dancing, lifting me in the air, kissing me again, dropping me on the floor on my ass like a sack of flour, and she keeping on dancing, turning this way, turning that way. Mother! What's going on? It had to be news of my father. I'd never seen her drink. Neither did I see her drink that night, no, she didn't drink, she just smelled of liquor, the whole house smelled of liquor, but she didn't drink, no, although she must have been drinking, I thought, and that dancing, it wasn't her style. But then she began to tell me what happened without losing the rhythm. Batista's out, two three, kick. Lotsa blood's already spilled, two, three, kick. Fidel's in, two, three, kick, a turn that way, salute, a turn the other way, everybody, Cuba libres down the hatch, two, three, kick. My first reaction was sad, on account of it wasn't news about my father, which I'd thought, a disappointment, and besides, what was this Batista to me, not my father. And then my mother picked up my Pocholo from the couch and began to dance with him, hugging him, whispering to him, and I jumped, no Mother, leave my Pocholo alone, I want to dance with him, she said, no, he's mine, but let him dance, I won't let him, and I pulled on him, selfish boy, but he's mine, until I ended up on the floor on my ass again, with half a

Pocholo in my hand, my mother banging face first into the wall with the other half, a little volcano of stuffing in the middle of the room, the rest flying around making us cough. Me not knowing whether to blame Batista, Fidel, or my mother.

Inevitable under the best of circumstances, inevitable. I hope it doesn't turn out to be a bad sign.

No, no, by no means. Now I have a girlfriend. My first.

Delightful. It was Stendhal who once described such a situation. But tell me yours.

Really? Are you interested?

A man is no more free of his past than he is of his body. Go ahead.

We met at a party I wasn't invited to and danced for quite a while. The next afternoon we met in Las Conchas Park, pure chance, as we hadn't planned it, I had no idea she was going to be there or if she wanted to see me again, she had a bored expression on her face the night before, and I doubt she would have planned it either but there she was, and we met. She said that she rarely went out, she took meeting me as a sign because she rarely went out, and invited me to her house. I accepted. It was a huge mansion, protected by a huge wall with huge spikes and huge electric cables and soldiers with huge machine guns, and to get in a huge door had to be opened. The walls of the house were made of cut glass from Bohemia, according to what she told me, and there was a fountain in the middle of a huge patio with flamingos standing around on one leg. We went on through underneath huge plants and a little artificial waterfall to her room, where she turned on the television. The walls were all mirrors reflecting us forever in ever direction. Then I saw the picture on the TV screen. It can't be, I said, without taking my eyes off it, it can't be because we don't have color television in this country. It's San Antonio, Texas, she said, yawning. We have a special aerial. My father would have a nervous breakdown if he couldn't see his football games on Sundays. And my mother once went out with Ed Sullivan. And me I didn't know what to say. And then she began taking her clothes off. She took everything off. And she lay down on the floor. There was a huge red rug on the floor, one sank into it, at least four inches thick and shaggy, and she lay down there hiding her hands under the desk and I looked at her and looked at her until she saw that I was looking at her and looking at her and she looked at me and I kept looking at her and she went on looking at me and I went on looking at her and then she made motions for me to sit down next to her on the rug. I kept on looking and she looked at me as though saying I should feel like this was my old stamping grounds. Or something of the kind. But I wasn't sure if I ought to strip too or if not and I said that I didn't like to watch television. No, no, she said, you sit down and look at me, not at the television. I look at the television. You wouldn't understand it anyway, she said, bursting out laughing, the announcers with faces like dummies talking as though they were gargling their throats, chungree, chungree, chungree, poor people to have to talk a language like that, I thought, and she kept on watching the screen, fascinated, and me by her. I didn't know, didn't dare, I just looked at her, like she told me to, hands in my pants pockets, eyes running over her spine from top to bottom, bam, bam, bam, bam, like going down a slide, until I came to the little tail bone, parararam, and then she stuck her tongue out at me. I jumped. She stretched and exerting a big effort managed to turn off the television. She turned toward me. Looked at me. What's your name? she asked. I told her. Too long, we folks don't like to talk long. It's tiring and there are more important things. I'll call you Max. I laughed. I like you, she said, you're cute, and I like to have you sitting here next to me. But don't be getting ideas. I'm a virgin. I laughed saying I was too. Her eyes sparkled and very excited she said that that was just what she had thought. You can look at me all you want. I like being looked at. But you can't do anything else unless I tell you to. Understand? Okay. I got up, leaned over the desk to look at her through the glass desk. Nothing blocked my view except two pencils in the drawer that practically formed a V without touching. She looked like a big white kitten stretched out on the rug waiting to be stroked and I noticed that I had left greasy finger marks on the very clean glass. I turned around to look at her reflection on the wall. She noticed, tilted her head to one side and closed her eyes. I'm beautiful, aren't I? And she wasn't bad, to tell the truth, she wasn't bad, the long strands of blonde hair making their way down to her bony heels. She stretched out her arms, whispering the abbreviation of my name. I sat on the floor, eyes fixed on the mirrors, she behind me in the center of the room, but in the reflection it seemed as though she was beside me and it was beautiful, beautiful, like that, next to me, the reflection. I blew her a kiss that turned into dense vapor on reaching the mirror, fogging over her image, obscuring it, her open mouth, her tongue, like a cobra's tongue, tempting me. I turned to look straight at her and she told me that I had to come and see her every Tuesday, Thursday, and Saturday after three. She reminded me that she was a virgin and served me tea and buttered toast.

Unbelievable. Truly unbelievable.

Something unbelievable, isn't it?

Unbelievable. Absolutely unbelievable.

Is it really that unbelievable?

It really is, really. But there's no reason to become prematurely concerned. There's no rush. But if you should feel the need, I know the right person. Her name is Amanda. But she's known as Amarena in professional circles. A good friend. Good. And I should add. Make sure to pay her a visit. I'll take you whenever you want. There's nobody better. No, sir.

Fine, thank you. Thanks for the offer. I mean it. It's that. I think that. I'd rather wait. Yes. See what happens. Know what I mean? There's time Yes. But. Well. Thank you. Anyhow. I mean it.

Just let me know. She's always prepared. Amarena. That's her slogan. Stole it from the Boy Scouts.

They entered the cantina. The wall peeling, covered with yellowed photos of forgotten saints, of old calendars, those suggestive photos, the air heavy with the heat. In one corner, the jukebox whining the last words of *The Treacherous Blow*. A chorus of words, voices scented with *Indita* following the trail of the melody through all the smoke, that crescendo of voices impossible to understand, threatening to break into a storm of discordant sounds. He remembered, yes, the Carmelite nuns devoutly intoning the national anthem and his eyes automatically half-shut to deter the sting of the smoke. A dead man stretched out beside the jukebox.

This is Chingolo, an apprentice thinker but he likes beer. Tip your hats and take no notice of his big nose.

Jeezus! Thinking and drinking are inseparable. What a fucked-up world. Sit down.

Thinking and drinking inseparable? I can see that, of course. Of course.

Chingolo felt Rodri's hand like a dead fish, Pacha's glasses steamed over. They sat. The pine table, poor table, so scarred and urgently in need of a coat of paint, conversation by grimaces, voices definitely inaudible, the jukebox.

> For your love that I want and need so much
> Pour me a drink and then many more
> Pour all at once for the rest of the year
> For I intend to get seriously drunk.

And the next day she forced him to go to the races. He felt embarrassed about her height but she was a blonde. Don't be stupid, she had told him on the way. With that top hat of yours we make a perfect couple.

What if I stand on the tails?

Nobody'll notice as long as your fly's not open.

He had never worn a coat in his life and felt funny in borrowed clothes. She carried a yellow parasol that matched her hair ribbon. The colors of her stable.

Was this love?

The stands superbly decorated. The walls covered with murals portraying biblical and classical subjects related to the event. Only famous painters had been commissioned such as the youngest of the Health Minister's 23 children. In the center of the stands facing east, the symbolic direction of the resurrection, the famous statue of the angel holding a beautiful stallion in the palm of its sacred hand. The spacious, beautifully built guillotine behind a circle of jacaranda trees pointing towards the mystical west. Padded with black velvet and two pillows of the same material to accommodate the shaky knees of the unfortunate occupant. A flag with his colors would be raised with all military honors. The police band conducted by its chubby leader with a curly mustache and a red baton. They had a double duty to perform. After the execution it was their task to keep the excited aristocrats from soaking their silk handkerchiefs in the blood.

Her horse was entered in the seventh race.

The bugle blew. The parade started to polite applause. Tons of dynamite inside glossy hides, the slender legs nervously twitching up and down, up and down, the sharpened edges of the hooves tracing cryptograms in the virgin sand.

I think I can take you to a volcano in eruption. A friend recommended Pacaya.

They had entered through the gate, one by one, reduced by the sunlight that was broiling the back stretch, scattered colors gleaming against the thick foliage. Mischievous drops of cold sweat on Karen's palms, disappearing down her wrists. Binoculars over her excited breast. A sigh, pushing aside the intruding elbow blocking her view. Unbearable heat.

They were off, and down the straightaway dots of color bouncing in the distance, fighting to escape the overpowering clouds of dust that grew, grew. Among the spectators, the crescendo of voices punctuated by sharp cries and the shaking of parasols. Go, boy! Powdered noses pointing ever skywards, nostrils dilating, gloved hands raised, waving. Look at him go! The silvered surface of the little artifical lake in the middle of the race track unruffled by a single wave, plumed hats bouncing up and down like a drowning man's head.

They were coming around the last turn when the horse fell. The crowd on their feet to a man, the strangled guttural outcry.

Hind legs brushing, hindquarters scraping, a whip dropped, a cap fallen. The two horses just behind the little body in yellow silks, unable to avoid it, the dust obscuring everything. In seconds they begin to emerge, one after another, the gray stallion out of the dust, the bay continuing its dash to the finish line behind the jet black mare. The dust beginning to settle. Like a riderless ghost steed, the horse trotting airily in shameful confusion.

His leg? Is it all right?

Color back in her face. Her head seeking the support of Máximo's shoulder, his arm, protective, hiding tears of desperation, exhausted relief following.

He's all right, Max, he's all right.

They went for a drink to assuage her parched throat. The race was over. The final order didn't matter to them. The horse was definitely all right. The trainer had already run to bring the good news. It was just that he had tripped. There were no torn ligaments, no broken bones. He would be ready for his next race, no question about it. He had been well in the lead when he fell. He'd win the next in a breeze.

But the jockey, Karen. He's dead, isn't he?

The jockey? That bay is worth its weight in gold. There aren't many like him even in Kentucky.

And they took their seats in the west stands to watch the execution of the losing jockeys. One by one they were led in pious solemnity by two hooded priests to the exquisite guillotine. The band played and the excited spectators drained the last of their French champagne. The jockeys elegantly divesting themselves of their humbled colors, shirts falling at their feet. In keeping with the ceremoniousness of the occasion all wore red T-shirts under their silks. So that their little bodies would not appear so offensively stained with the blood. The priests recited the appropriate litanies, the executioner impassively awaiting the signal.

If we had brought in the jockey I wanted. He would never have fallen, Max, I know.

Enough! They are human beings, too. That's real blood.

He stood up, smiled. He patted her on the head absently, smiling. And went towards the closest exit, all eyes on him, not losing his smile, she watching him open-mouthed, what right did he have, if that was the tradition, what humiliation, what would people say? He was going through the exit when she finally stood up.

Max waited.

He waited. She was upset, her corsage danger-ously close to falling off and her makeup stained with perspiration.

But Máximo was sufficiently calmed down three days later to take her to Pacaya. She picked wild-flowers in a cool glade surrounded by evergreens, he seated on a rock telling gory stories and playing all the time with her artificial ear. They climbed to the crater after lunch. She threw the flowers into the lava watching with great pleasure as they disappear-ed totally the instant they touched the boiling liquid that sent up red clouds. As though they had never been there. Máximo tickling her and she threatening to throw his pacifier into the crater. Descending late in the afternoon, he thinking, would thirteen be the appropriate age for losing it? The light filtered by between the growing shadows of the trees whose branches danced over their heads. He liked those little wrinkles that formed at the sides of her nose when she smiled. There was a faint odor of eucalyptus in the air and all was tranquil.

Nobody loves me. I don't mean a thing to anybody. I'm going out and eat caterpillars. Yesterday I ate a hairy one, today I'll eat a green one.

Mother! All I did was remind you that you promised to tell me more about my father. I just would like to know. And you promised to.

What father? What father? Not my father. What father?

Mine, mother. Mine.

Know something, son? It's time for another revolution. I was talking about just that point with some very interesting ladies there on the beach. The thing to do is to follow the example of the Cubans, clean out the gringos...

Mother! That's not what-I-was-ask-ing-you.

You have no faith in the guerrillas, then?

Shit, can't a person get a straight answer around here?

Watch your language! Just watch your language!

He would have strangled her but the bell rang. He picked up his windbreaker and slammed the door. Chingolo didn't say a word. He walked alongside Máximo, bicycle over his shoulder.

My mother has always been impossible but lately she's driving me absolutely up the wall. Now she's latched onto the revolution, that the time is now and everything stinks, that she wants to go marching behind a regiment of beards.

It is getting serious, finally. Peralta Absurdo has a lot of dead men at his door but the guerrilla is loose, Luis Turcios is loose and the generals are purple in the face, worse than that, black.

It's not that, man.

What, then?

She refuses to talk about my father. We've fought over that since the day I learned to talk. All I want to know is a few facts. His name, for example. What the hell he looked like, if he had birthmarks, or a beard. How he disappeared, if they killed him, if he had pimples on his forehead. She won't talk. What she's hiding, I just don't know. But every once in a while she promises to tell me more, mentions that it's important for me to know, and then never does it, and I have to remind her, and then she raises the roof with me, and me lying awake nights thinking, thinking, what the fuck could have happened. But if I bring it up she gives me the business about my having no consideration. How can I cope with that kind of thing?

Kill her, ignore her, or skip.

Big help you are.

Booze. Love and drink to drown your sorrows.

I'm serious, man.

Become an artist. Beauty is an escape for some.

Come on. What I want is an answer.

Escape your present. Ignore it, transcend it, mock the vastness of eternity.

Ignore it?

Explore it.

Deplore it?

Implore it.

Abhor it.

I'm with you. You've won my respect.

You don't say? And what can I do with it. Hock it?

If you want to. Everything's possible. Governing and giving orders are different arts, too, that must be kept in mind.

Always bullshitting.

No, I'm serious. Seriousness is one of the hallmarks of my being. Were you by any chance aware that you are the seventh member of the human race without a male progenitor to have entered my amicatory circle?

You mean without an old man? No, I was not.

The other six disappeared on them, too, under the bombs. It was quite a popular thing in those days, to do a Houdini between one blast and the next.

That's what they say. But do you really know that many?

Haven't I told you that seriousness is my hallmark?

I never ran into another.

Because you are still a beardless boy. But one who lived through it. All were good pals here and there in that mythical temporal straightaway. Some know what happened to their progenitors, however, just as I know where my nose went or, rather, where it came from. One was ripped open by a bomb. Another was put up against the wall because, they say, he made eyes at Colonel Castle Cannons. Another is in Cuba.

Fidel's Cuba?

Is there another? Can you buy cubas on the street two for five with salt and pepper?

No, man, it's just that it sounds so unreal, as distant as Olympus. That real people live there and that one of them is the old man of somebody you know is like knowing a person who won the lottery.

In other words, you would be interested pursuing your life on that island?

Well, could be, I don't know.

No? You don't know? Do you have any doubts in your heart? Go ahead, let me hear.

I don't know if my father is there, it never occurred to me before.

So what? What's the difference? Who cares? What do you care? Why should you care? Who should care? What? What?

Hey, what do I know?

What do I know? Maybe you think the beards are just a fad like the miniskirt or the twist.

Right now I just want to know about my old man, okay?

Seeking your identity, by the corns of old Seneca, the teenager in you now comes out. Didn't anybody ever tell you that is a tired old idea?

The bombs held me back.

Sure. True child of underdevelopment that you are, you come late to the party. But leave the breast-beating to the church biddies, man. Outworn illusions must be destroyed. You must create a nice new set for yourself, find yourself a new dream. If you get really serious you paralyze yourself and you're screwed.

They knocked on a door. A pair of huge black eyes, who's there, through the little window in the middle of the door. Chingolo explained. The door swung open. The eyes of the butler who turned imperiously to lead them through the labyrinth of the great house. Chingolo amused himself explaining to Máximo obscure architectural features of the building that attested to its antiquity. Holding forth as well on the tremendous variety of exotic plants that adorned the patio. The butler hearing without listening. He led them to the last, enormous, dark room, its walls in gold, reds, and blues. Two elegant replicas of antique oil lamps stood on the night table flanking the widest bed Máximo had ever seen. Completely covered by a vast gold bedspread, pillows everywhere, cushions, cushions of all sizes, gigantic cushions strewn about the room. He could see that the rug was of llama skin. The woman was sitting in the middle of the bed, her feet tucked up under her, brushing her extremely long hair with her left hand, her enormous brown eyes fixed on his. She wore a low-cut nightgown intricately embroidered in silver. Her skin was dark but her face with its finely chiseled nose and delicate upper lip betrayed her as a foreigner.

Amarena! *Darleeng*! What a joy to behold you once more...

You did like it, didn't you, old man, but always play hard to get.

She had a very slight accent tripping softly and exquisitely from her lips. Máximo unable to tear his gaze from that almost transparent nightgown. She was young, beautiful, voluptuously formed.

I bring you a new chum to play with. I'm showing him around, extending his sphere of knowledge, expanding his sensitivity.

Máximo laughed, feeling a fool, aware of being given away by his flushed face. She laughed gently, without mockery, the tip of her tongue peeping from between her slightly parted lips.

He's a virgin.

Ah, the way I like them best.

I could have killed Chingolo at that moment if I had had a knife, without hesitation, without saying I'm sorry.

I was telling him before about how beauty provides a means of escape.

She laughed, an open laugh full of vitality, completely natural, Máximo following the sway of her tremulous breasts. She was addressing him.

Did you ever hear the saying: He who tries woman finds ruin?

And laughing again, Chingolo with her. He could have killed them both, yes, her, too, breasts and all.

He has a little girlfriend, however, and you'll never guess who, dearest. None other than Karen Johnson.

No! Not possible? *The* Karen Johnson? Don Maximiliano's daughter?

The same.

And she turned toward him again, processing the new information, inspecting him, head to foot, hands on her hips, head to foot again, slowly.

You don't say!

Do you know her?

Do I know her? Ay, sonny, I see her every Sunday, we have conversed *so many* times after services?

What services?

Religious services. At the Union Church. Didn't you know, my father is the minister of the Union Church?

He didn't know. He knew what the Union Church was. The city's Protestant church, exclusively for the gringo colony. Although they did allow the British and Scots in, and people of that kind. Right in the Plazuela España, opposite the Charles III fountain and the Monsanto Building. And the only church in the country with electric bells that play a song all set up beforehand and not hit or miss like the bells that call to mass.

Take care now you don't faint. I'll bet you've never seen a minister's daughter before.

My mother hates priests. But I'm a Catholic anyway and it's hard to get to know priests' daughters.

Don't worry. We're nicer people than the Mormons. Come here. Come closer.

He came to the edge of the bed. She leaned over. Took the pacifier out of his mouth gently and holding it in her right hand, began to stroke it, the pacifier, lovingly with her fingers, those silken fingers, the pacifier coated with saliva, stroking it, on its sides, gently, upwards then downwards, gently, smiling, smiling.

She can teach you what to do with Karen Johnson.

Don't tell me even that has to be learned.

Does it have to be learned? Máximo! Everything in life is an ardent learning process, you know that. In order that we may function as one with nature, as Bacon said. *Ars est homo additus naturae*! It is necessary to learn to play with the elements nature has provided us with in rough form in order to satisfy the emerging demands of the soul!

She slid the moist pacifier over her chest, slowly, between her breasts, as though she had forgotten he was there, that Chingolo was there. Unbelievable. She played with the pacifier like a little boy with a toy automobile, over one breast, over the other, between them. She raised her eyes, looking at him. She winked, bent over towards him, passed her hand over his fly.

If the human spirit hadn't in the course of the centuries learned to play, our love affairs would be nothing more than sexual gymnastics! Walk through parks, follow the course of rivers, and observe the animals of the air! Watch how they do it and then go home and read *Discours sur les Passions de l'Amour* so that you may gauge the gulf that exists in love between art and nature!

She with the pacifier in her mouth slowly sucking it, she was sucking it, moving it from right to left, left to right, eyes shut, the sound of breathing, that long-drawn-out sound.

As though by magic, two miserable procreations of anybody at all, fragile as any, selfish as we also are by nature, timid, without faith, savages, evolved into one of the most intimate and delightful of communions.

She leaned over to whisper something, her hand on his fly, licking his ear.

You'll never regret having gotten your start with me. I'm Amarena to you. That's what all my friends call me. I insist.

But it's that I... what with your father... I don't know... And you so tall that...

But I'm very good. What difference does a couple of inches make? It's not the size that counts but the movement of the hips.

He snatched the pacifier from her mouth, putting it into his own, grabbed his windbreaker from the chair, ran out into the hall pulling up the zipper of his fly, misjudging the distance, knocked over a pot of begonias, turned to see the extent of the damage, the laughter coming out of the room, banged into a column, the laughter tumbling to the ground, rising, he got up dazed, the laughter rising, continuing his flight, he ran, looking desperately for the front door.

But despite that cauliflower face of his, Peralta Absurdo managed to remain in power, trembling at those guerrillas that wouldn't disappear, that didn't go away. Washington bursting with pride. His courage, his stalwartness. Such daring. They promised to keep him in power unless something really unusual happened. Peralta Absurdo stepped up to the podium to give his state-of-the-nation message. He promised to have plastic surgery done the following year. He received an ovation from the church biddies.

Towards the end of the week Máximo had recovered enough to accept going out with Karen in her capacious limousine. There was a huge moon and the trees were loaded with sweet-smelling fruit but she had a headache. Why don't we get out and walk in the park, he suggested. She reminded him how dangerous it was to get out of the limousine. The butchers were on strike and had kidnapped the Archbishop's sexton. The soldiers were prowling the streets and they weren't vaccinated against rabies. Cars were searched. Curfew had been moved back to 10 p.m. Armed guerrillas still around Oriente and ambitious colonels attacking with napalm, machine-gunning cattle, and then landing for the picnic. The Minister of Defense: Those missions a great victory. Monsanto a gold mine selling more and more napalm. And a new plane was on the way with technical advisers bearing gifts. Why endanger diplomatic immunity by getting out? When it was a bulletproof vehicle.

To be able to gauge the gulf that exists in love between art and nature.

Where did you pick up that crap?

He won the argument. They got out of the car. They sat down under the great cypress with long branches and listened to the call of the owl. Máximo leaned his back up against the tree trunk and she rested her head on his outstretched legs. They could hear the sound of a stream running below. In the depths of the ravine. Las Conchas was a lovely park. In the heart of that very wealthy sector of the city, the wealthiest probably. With paths going down to the stream and leading upwards again. He told her how Chingolo was telling him that in their countries they had to latch onto whatever in order to prevent total stagnation. That very generalized paralysis already mentioned.

Is your friend a Communist?

Karen, really!

They went down to the stream, holding hands, avoiding the slime-covered puddles, breathing in the humid breeze perfumed by the pines. They saw a huge green lizard on a boulder. The placid stream emerging from behind the shrubbery and crossing to the left. Then they saw the first body going by right in front of them, in silence. Naked, and where could he have lost his head, his hands? Karen and Máximo looked at each other. It passed by. And it hadn't yet disappeared to the left when the next one came along on the other side. Floating face up. It was a man, you could tell though there was nothing to tell by. Resting tranquilly now without penis or testicles. The water beginning to stain inevitably red. Let's get out of here.

They climbed as fast as they could. Hands bathed in cold sweat. His forehead, breast, armpits quivering. Máximo turned just as two more floated by.

I thought you, at least, would be used to it.

Look who's talking, shitty gringa, didn't you enjoy seeing the heads roll at the Jockey Club?

That's different. They lost the race. And besides the ceremony was being strictly followed.

He dropped her arm and went off along another path. The way to school. He remembered her sweater, in his other hand, and left it hanging on the end of a branch. She ran after him.

What's the matter with you?

I'm walking home.

Oh, you Latins, you're all impossible. What's bugging you, now?

One learns. And on learning, the game of sticking it out starts. Until you can't stick it out any longer.

He reached the sidewalk and walked in the direction away from the parked car. She still trailing after him. He crossed the street, turned the corner, stopped at the lamp post to catch his breath. He closed his eyes. When he opened them again she was standing before him, laughing nervously.

Let's go back to the house, dummy. You live too far away.

Thanks. I'm sick of ceremony.

Okay. We can discuss it in the car. Come on.

She took him by the hand and on turning the corner a group of six men with machine guns stopped them.

Your ID's if you don't mind.

She answered that they didn't have any ID's on them, that they had left them in the glove compartment of the limousine. They didn't believe her. She said that she was telling them the truth, that the car was parked just a couple of blocks away. They didn't believe her. She told them that her father was acting ambassador besides being president of

Monsanto, and that he had diplomatic immunity. They didn't believe her. She told them that if they touched her Peralta Absurdo would personally blow their brains out. They didn't believe her. She told them that a new plane would be landing any minute with technical advisers who would track them to the ends of the world if they touched her. They didn't believe her. She said that this was enough nonsense and that they should go to the limousine where the chauffeur would tell them. They didn't believe her.

They wanted to check her purse to make sure that the ID wasn't in it. She became enraged. But okay, she said, and threw it at them. One of the men picked it up and began going through it while another one raised his machine gun threateningly. No ID here, the man said, pocketing all the money he found. They were going to have to search them. She shouted that they'd better be careful, how dare they, that she herself would chop their heads off on the Jockey Club guillotine. But the man said that it was the law. She yelled that it wasn't curfew yet but he answered that they were blocking traffic. A third man agreed and suggested that they cross the street and go into the park to settle the matter. He said that he refused to move a step until they apologized to her but they pointed their machine guns at his head. She shouted that she wasn't moving from there and dared them to shoot. They pointed their machine guns at her head. He said that if they promised to treat her with respect they both would go to the park. The men agreed, jiggling their fingers around the triggers. They crossed the street with the men around them and went some distance into the park. They stopped and one of the men ordered the search to begin. He protested and the other man said that it was their duty to enforce the law. He had one man in front of him and one in back and she the same. A third man approached him and began going through his pockets. After searching his side pockets, he dug into the back pocket of his trousers and the breast pocket of his shirt. The other man told him to check the cuffs of his trousers but he found nothing there either. When he approached her, she began to scream and another one had to come and hold her arms behind her back. The man checked the pockets of her skirt and since she had no back pockets, he went through the ones in her blouse as she screamed. No ID, he said. All right, then, said the other. Since they refuse to cooperate with the law, we'll have to make a more thorough search. Strip them. The two screamed louder than ever but there was nothing they could do. One man unbuttoned his shirt and another his trousers. He tried to kick him but received a slap in the testicles. He saw that they had not done anything to her yet. He asked if anybody had some Vicks, saying he needed a little for his nose. They told him they would give him a scholarship to Panama if he didn't shut up. They tore his shirt off and handed it to another to be gone through, then his trousers and shorts were passed over to the same hands. He felt cold but could see the sweat running down his body and that they were still holding on to her but she was no longer screaming and was being forced to watch what they were doing to him. He asked what a scholarship to Panama was. They guffawed and forced him to open his mouth while another shoved his fingers down his throat and he felt the nausea rising and as the man removed his hand two streams of vomit appeared at the corners of his mouth. They lifted his penis to see if he had anything concealed there and the same with his testicles. They turned him around and two of them separated his buttocks while a third stuck his fingers into his anus. No ID he said. He realized he was crying and had been for a while without knowing it but then they opened her blouse. She began screaming again and kicking and he tried to tell her not to but couldn't find his voice. One man slapped her belly and she spit at him. The man struck her in the breasts a couple of times. They had ripped her blouse off and and another was fumbling for the fastener of her bra. They were trembling more and more and a few were sweating almost as much as he was. Her bra was on the ground and her panties were coming off but she had stopped shrieking and kicking. She did nothing. Like a rag doll. They pushed her to the ground and opened her mouth while one stuck his fingers deep inside. He saw that she was weeping, the tears streaming from her eyes but not a sob could be heard, only her chest rising and falling, they pinching her breasts and turning her artificial ear around and around. They raised her legs in the air with one of the men astride her belly and kept forcing them forward until her feet were almost touching her ears. The man stuck his fingers into her anus, and surprised not to find anything, tried again. No ID, he said. Another volunteered to hold her labia apart as they laughed at her blonde pubic hair. The man began to push his fingers into her vagina. She's a virgin, he said. She's a virgin, the others shouted. One of them turned to ask him if he was a virgin, too. There was no answer and the man pulled out his truncheon and hit him on the back. Yes, yes, he began to shout and felt a stick prodding his testicles. The men looked at one another and asked them how old they were. Thirteen, he said. She said nothing. She didn't even seem to know that she was being asked a question. The man with the truncheon struck her on the ass. She screamed and her eyes were enormous but the question remained unanswered. The club struck her again. After the third blow she managed to yell that she was thirteen, too, before vomiting. One of the men said that they were very old to be virgins and that something should be done about it. The others were all in agreement. The man told him to get it up but he kept his eyes closed. The truncheon caught him in the back and the man shouted that if he didn't get it up in five minutes he would cut it off. He yelled that he couldn't, he couldn't. They let go of his right hand so that he could use it to help. But meanwhile the men took turns kissing her on the breasts to enhance the beauty of the experience. They discussed the point that a lot of kisses were necessary the first time and decided to kiss her clitoris to help her along even more. One of the men suggested that perhaps somebody with more experience should service her the first time and he volunteered. But the others opposed, arguing that it would be unfair for just one to have to go through it. They were all equal, as the laws of democracy required, and it was better to let the youngsters work it out themselves. He failed to be ready in the time he had been allotted but was given an extension. This unexpected situation allowed them time to help her along some more. The second time limit expired and he still wasn't ready. One of the men took a large feather and began helping him with it. The man moved in closer, and closer. Finally, he succeeded. Finally, they all said, and they lifted her in the air as they held him firmly down on the ground. Opening her legs they sat her politely over the waiting member, carefully, to make sure the parts met properly. One of the men held the penis at attention. They let her down by the shoulders and thighs and she submerged slowly giving vent to the loudest howls any of them had ever heard, but he didn't want to hear the screams, didn't want to hear them. When finally he was all the way into her, she had fainted and one of the men ran to the stream for water to bring her to. She didn't seem to be reviving so they struck her repeatedly with the truncheon and then she fainted again. They got angry and pushed her head against his and turned them over so that he would end up on top of her. They drew two more truncheons and began to beat him on the back, thighs, legs, shoulders, and ribs. He was twisting with pain and their excitement mounted with the acceleration of his movements. He moaned and they slapped each other on the back with satisfaction and passed out cigarettes. And then they sat on the ground to contemplate the drops of blood that ran down her thighs. He had stopped twisting and one of the men got up to work him over a little more with his truncheon while another hit him in the testicles. He yelled, no, no, and they told him to keep twisting if he wanted them to stop beating him. Twist, twist, twist! The man stopped hitting him and he kept writhing. Twist, twist, twist! The twist was in fashion at the time! Twist, twist, twist! They enjoyed their smoke and reminisced nostalgically about their first love experiences and he kept twisting, kept twisting. First love, said one of them with a sigh. There's nothing like it.

CHAPTER 5

REVELATIONS

We were in a big canoe. The rapids very rough. Jungle down to the river's edge. Dense jungle, dark, thick with mangroves along the banks. It could have been the Pasión or Usumacinta but in my dream it was a river on the southern coast. We were fighting to keep afloat and realized that it was already six o'clock and growing dark. We looked up just in time to catch sight of a big bamboo hut near the water. And all at once there we were sitting in a passageway. Night had fallen and two Indians, faces hard as stone, were watching us. One of them asked my father what we had in our knapsacks and my father looked at me. Neither of us answered. But I took note of the size of their machetes. They gave us a room to sleep in and my father blew out the candle. I could see the flickering flame in my dream. But we were awakened by shouts. Father, I called out, and ran for my boots. Father, that shouting! I couldn't see him any longer but still felt his presence in the shadows. And then they were chasing us and I saw the machetes gleaming in the moonlight. Making my way through the undergrowth I reached the river, jumped in, and began to swim downstream. But I was alone by then. I had been sensing his presence less and less. I was alone. Swimming like a solitary alligator on the clear surface of the vast, deep, mysterious river, floating eternally downstream. And now it was no longer possible to recall his face. It was a secret, it was nothing. But I knew it was he, just as I knew that those were not really Indians chasing us even though I had seen the machetes and recognized the hostility of their expressions when we were sitting in the passageway.

Chingolo said nothing. Máximo waited. Chingolo chased off a fly buzzing around his nose, looked up at the sky, scratched his back, said that the post office had returned his collective unconscious unopened. Apparently for insufficient postage.

Shit, shouted Máximo. Like talking to the wall. And he left him watching the crazy people doing calisthenics. To go to Amarena. She was more substantial. Unpretentious, unambitious, straight to the heart of things.

But she was out. The new government that had ousted General Peralta Absurdo cancelled the official roster for whores. They immediately called a strike. Amarena volunteered. To help organize. He had asked her what for. What for? she had answered in amazement. Well, because one shouldn't just close one's eyes and do nothing. Action had to be taken. In everything. Against everything.

Three years had passed.

Máximo wanted to forget. Máximo wasn't able to forget. Her face appeared to him in the air, transparent, looking at him. It came by in places where he least expected, talking softly to him. He went to play soccer and there it would be. He saw it as he went from bar to bar. He had attended a funeral a few days before. He saw her on the corner of Liberty and Lies. Of course, it had also appeared to him at Amarena's house. But worst of all. It began taking over the few, abashed pages he was finally scribbling. Would it ever go away?

Chingolito, *darling*, how is the sentimental education of your new disciple progressing?

Groggily. Opening his little eyes halfway, lash by lash.

Máximo decided that it was too early to go home and confront his mother. He returned to the crazies' park. Chingolo was no longer there. What difference did it make? The whores were preparing for their demonstration. So many were already assembled that they blocked the crazy people from view. A well-developed one was protesting indignantly over the public address system. Máximo recognized Amarena among the group by her mink coat. He shouted goodbye to her and disappeared down a forgotten alley.

Three years.

From the hospital straight to the airport. Her father with her. Very early the next morning the ships were already seen approaching, without tears, where sky and ocean meet. Peralta Absurdo, enraged, livid, desperately sending message after message to Washington. The army on general alert. There wasn't a soul to be seen on the streets. Total curfew was in force. Twenty-four hours a day.

Everybody heard the distant shots that night. The criminals had been dragged before the firing squad and executed forthwith, Peralta Absurdo said.

His last message to the nation. Justice again triumphant, he said. But nobody had asked Máximo to identify them, to bear witness to their monstrous smiles. Nobody knew who he was, he was invisible. The heads were cut off their bodies and sent to Washington as proof. The night was unbearably hot and it seemed that a downpour was on its way but no rain at all fell that night.

The following day all the ships had dropped anchor in the ports. The helicopters were frightening the vultures in the sky. Dollars began circulating freely in the night clubs. The new head of state was General Arriando el Bosque. But to keep up appearances Major W.A."Pappy" Shelton had an obscure lawyer of dubious credentials with a Roman emperor's name sworn in as president. It is important, Don Pappy had said. To support democratic principles. Watch your step about daring to flout the general. The Archbishop was there, shaking hands with Peralta Absurdo, wishing him a pleasant vacation in Miami. And due to the unrest arising from the change of administration schools would be closed for the following year.

And when do you think the boy is going to get over his fear, Chingolito?

When anger successfully routs it, my little love.

And a survey was made by the new government. Endless lists appeared. There would be a knock and on opening the door you found yourself face to face with a machine gun that said good morning. Offering a soft drink not obligatory. The official would explain the importance of accurate statistics in this technological age. You would be invited to answer a few questions. You would look into the eye of the machine-gun barrel and say, of course, at your service. The official, proud of the cooperation on the part of the citizenry. Democracy in action. Everything was very formal.

Do you approve of the present government? Yes? No? Undecided? Do you consider civil revolution necessary? Yes? No? Undecided? Do you admire Fidel Castro? Yes? No? Undecided? Have you ever considered communism acceptable? Has any member of your family? Relations? Pets? Do you agree that peasant and workers' organizations are an obstacle to the nation's economic development? Did you feel emotion when you heard that the heroes of the Bay of Pigs had been trained in our country? This was a difficult question. The type of emotion felt had to be specified. Did you...? Did you...? Did...?

Careful thought was necessary to answer properly. All kinds of factors had to be considered. The conscientious citizen took the survey seriously.

Tell what he does for a pastime, tell.

He's constantly asking me crazy questions until he can't stand my answers any longer. Then he goes away, I don't know where.

Would Máximo be able to write? To explain what had happened. To understand. To try to get hold of himself, yes. To perhaps make the face that pursues him, that gives him no peace, vanish. And failing that to establish dialogue with it. He had begun to write in strictest secrecy, hiding on suspicious corners, always alert to hide his pencils at the first sound of footsteps, determined to keep them from being seen. It was his private shame, his way of fighting, of negating that real-life experience. Of getting revenge. His mother suspected that he had begun to masturbate.

It was not enough, it wasn't at all. The face refusing to disappear. He continued his long strolls with Chingolo along interminable streets. Chingolo would talk and talk. And Máximo happily paying him no attention checking out the whores who were collecting signatures for a petition. Máximo decided it was time to buy a parrot. It was impossible to write without a parrot, a green one, how write without it? Chingolo informing him meanwhile that according to the most recent scientific research in the most advanced foreign universities, a cat that purrs is a happy cat.

Enthusiasm was insufficient. The words refused to cooperate. Skittish. They wouldn't approach. He was desperate and his allergy threatened to break out again. His face was not healing, the other face pursuing him. He decided that he must read more but couldn't stand the whiteness of the pages.

Máximo told Chingolo that he did not resent the tyranny of desire over reason. He was quite satisfied that it should be that way. He had checked through his memory and recalled the old man who told him his first story. He had recalled the last words of the first writer he met. Never would he be able to forget his initiation into love. He had checked through lists of generals and soccer games. He had thought about volcanoes and old age. Cantinas, trees, and mountains, and a lake here and there. He had considered every state, cogitated and meditated. And the word *reason* slipped away from each and every one of the objects like a thief about to be caught redhanded. We should let it go, he said to Chingolo.

Let it go and bother foreigners, Russians, gringos, Europeans. Aha, shouted Chingolo leveling an accusing finger at him. And Máximo had to confess that he was already feeling very strongly attracted to metaphor.

Chingolo was satisfied. He bought him a double-dip vanilla ice cream and patted him on the head. He told him how Thomas Mann had spent entire nights without sleep seeking answers to questions without answers. He said that Chekhov had done the same.

Máximo decided to adopt them as his teachers and to try to do the same. He would spend entire nights without sleep. Worried. By daybreak he would be a better writer. In a few weeks, maybe months, he would be ready to begin a book. He asked himself why more people didn't write. But then he remembered the bonfire.

But the face would not leave him alone, no, no, it wouldn't leave him. The face, the mutilated body, all of her: his Karen. That image. She riding on the back of the motorcycle with her very obliging friend. That image would not leave him. He had by now forgotten whether Saint Louis or some other saint. The name, the distant city where it happened. She must have been wearing trousers, tight trousers. And her bare arms around his waist, all that blonde down caressed by the wind from the prairie, her waxen arms. She would be wearing a pair of boots, gliding over the pavement like a raindrop on a silken leaf and just as unconscious. Perhaps thinking about him, how could she forget him? And surely she never saw the truck.

Did you know that our child prodigy writes?

You don't say? Come, climb up here alongside me, don't be stuffy.

Just think of it, losing yourself in words.

He's coming along, man. He's beginning to do something, to react. Don't be a pain, come on up here, just leave him alone.

One night, after downing a considerable number of *Inditas*, Máximo confessed to Pacha and Rodri that he had begun writing. And Rodri told him that they were also considering an exploration trip to Mayan ruins. Brother! All the layers of knowledge in the Mayan ruins, he said. They are old, really old. An established reference point. Tall and angular. Representing countless myths. But best of all, he added, they were far, very far away. Difficult to get to, if not impossible. Far? Yes, I see, sure, said Pacha. Far enough away to excite the imagination, said Rodri. But just imagine how swollen your feet will be when you get there, said Máximo. Brother! Look at how they've swelled from all the soccer here, said Rodri. And he agreed. But at least you get to play, said Máximo. You can play any time and almost any place, even though you abuse your feet.

The first night he tried the Thomas Mann method, he lasted until midnight before falling asleep. The second time he made it till 2:25. He was still young.

News from the north had filtered down slowly, changing direction constantly like the wind, but it kept arriving, arriving regularly, good news, bad news, finding its way over deserts, mountains, through virgin jungle, to the lost cities of the south. Finally reaching Máximo. She had already been in the hospital for two months. Impossible to save her

124

right leg. How sad this last made him. Now her warmth, her weight, only memories filtering dark thoughts. How beautiful, how soft, time's inevitable distortion had made her for him. Those hard consonants, Ka-ren. Ka-ren, sweetened in passing those moistened lips.

In the morning, the front pages informed the people that the country was on the verge of civil war. He drank a glass of orange juice to give him strength for when the war came. His mother, on a hunger strike.

It's gotten worse, mother, you're right. My friend Chingolo has been telling me a bunch of stuff I never even imagined. Growing resistance against the government. The jails packed. The other day, even the corner druggist ended up in the jug, nobody even knows why, but they say because his laundress had sold some joints to a soldier and, on account of it the jerk shot Colonel Búscame y Encuéntrame on the right cheek of his ass, thinking it was Comandante Turcios. And ambassadors are being kidnapped every day. To the point where recently a group of so-called leftists was on the way back from the mountain with the Ambassador of Lower Volta when a group of so-called rightists kidnapped them all smack on the road, after which nearly an hour went by before they were kidnapped themselves by another group of so-called leftists who fortunately set the black man free. People falling dead on the streets. Where I don't know, because personally I've yet to see one fall but they must pick them up right away or maybe it's that I got so accustomed to seeing corpses as a child that I don't even notice. But, anyway, I'm getting disaccustomed, now. The guerrilla movement is growing. The right keeps on killing on every corner. Arriando el Bosque personally directed the Mano Blanca death squads although he goes around bragging how clean his hands are because he has his eye on the Big Chair. The Archbishop came out in the paper today announcing that if anybody kidnaps him not to forget to bring his little portable radio so he won't miss the soap he's following. And guess what else. School will be closed for the coming year.

Máximo recalled how one night he tried to cheer Karen up by making indiscreet remarks about the dangers of capitalism. To tell the truth that mattered little to him in those days. And laughing, she led him by the hand to the door. It's not fair, he was yelling. Who said it was, she answered, and slammed the door in his face.

One Sunday afternoon, Máximo, Pachi, and Rodri were taking a walk kicking empty cans along the way and claiming that they were looking for meaning, for explanations. The whores appeared at the corner with placards painted red, lined up eight deep. Máximo remembered that the road to Xibalbá was one way on Monday, Wednesday, and Friday and the other way on Tuesday, Thursday, and Saturday. But nothing was said about Sunday. The whores marched down the street waving their signs, chorusing their demands, and twisting their parasols to the rhythm of their high heels clicking on the pavement. They came by in impressive numbers and turned left further on. Máximo was waiting to wave to Amarena. She came by blowing him a kiss and shouting to him that she was taking action. Pacha and Rodri were impressed. He wanted to blush but the blood wouldn't rise to his face. He tried to concentrate his thoughts on the ancestors of the common bean.

He tried the Thomas Mann system again that night. Chingolo had not specified what was worrying Mann. Answers to questions that had no answer sounded a little too general to him. But was Chingolo able to give him a more specific answer? He'd have to do what he could. He began to worry about what should be worrying him. Should he be worried about Amarena who had gotten slightly tear-gassed? Should he worry about his father? Well, he had been worrying about him for so long that it didn't really matter anymore. But he could be worried about pressuring his mother to tell him more. He wanted to know what the world was like before the bombs. There, that was it? Now he knew, few things interested him more than that. Well, one or two other small matters, maybe.

There was that other face. But that in general. He had to worm it out of his mother, worm it out of his mother

But the face started in again. Damned if I can get it out of my mind. And he started brooding about it all over again. Would she have been laughing? Would she have pouted, poking her lower lip all the way out. Did she frown, those thick eyebrows forced into two perfect arcs. Her nose? Would she stick the pink little tip of her tongue out for a fleeting second? What did she do when those long fingers of hers slipped like melted butter over the curves in her new stump. Did she miss the goose bumps on her knee, the titillating sensation of the shaved little hairs when she would slide her hand over her calf, over her bony heel.

Time passed and passed, Máximo trying to master the art of not sleeping. There was nothing better for the purpose than memories of Karen. Bad news from the north years before, bad and worsening, and from bad to worse, life. The artificial leg rejected by the stump. Modifications had to be made. More operations. The skin sensitive, reacting against every change, allergies like the ones he had suffered, chapping, pus. Increasing pain, the skin refusing to cooperate. Days came and days went and she in her wheelchair watching the muscles shrink, the swelling grow, perhaps nurturing sweet thoughts to distract the missing member.

Máximo visited Amarena when she had to take to her bed after receiving an overdose of tear gas. Her vivacity was truly refreshing. Even though inevitably she abashed him. She enjoyed it. It brought back bitter memories but gradually, very gradually, the play element began to dominate. How she loved zippers and he, talking, standing at the edge of the bed, she sitting, legs crossed and, all at once, the zipper up and down, and biting harder on his pacifier, feeling with horror his trousers stretching tighter and tighter. She always served him lemonade and wore the same transparent nightgown. She adored being looked at.

Three years had elapsed since the unforgettable experience at Las Conchas park.

And they'd talk and talk, about whether the police would dare shoot, if there would be more dead, about a benefit dance for the strikers, how she would try to talk her father into giving it a plug at the Union Church, only too well aware of the consequences. She insinuating — seriously? — that the whores were the strongest social group in the entire country.

Máximo remembered. He had heard the news exactly one year after she had gone. Her powers of reckoning had impressed him. Such preciseness. Like a good gringa, after all. He was going to Pacaya with Chingolo. To get away from the rain that had been coming down for the last six days. Chingolo obsessed with proving a theory on the composition of color in boiling lava and Máximo going along to keep him from falling into it. And then came the news. Suddenly, the picture blacker, soggier, unbearable, constrictive, vomitive. Not that he reacted. His mind a blank. They went to Pacayá and Chingolo was the one who had to hold him up. Him. Unbecoming a gentleman, he had told him. And he insisted that he sit on a rock while he conducted his experiments, at the risk of his nose. Máximo remembering. He sat there, unaware of time, asking himself what catastrophic forces could have swept her away, to what heights her pain could have reached that those tires should have become her only escape.

He had never been there. Would it be possible one day? Was it Saint Louis after all? He had never been out of the country. What was it like abroad. But he certainly would see that house, her house. The big living room with its modern Danish furnishings. She sitting on the edge of that enormous red couch agonizingly sporting the latest attempt at a new leg. The other three sitting there with her. One of them, the tall blond guy with the close haircut. She looking at him. Bragging about the tremendous power of his new Honda. And she taking it all in, eyes wide, not saying anything other than that they should go to the kitchen for more beer, watching them disappear in that whiteness. And then?

They knowing nothing. Lost in the noise of meaningless conversation. Until the sound of the motor was heard shattering all peace. What had happened? What had gone through her mind in that briefest infinity that found her desperately alone? What reserve of vitality did she have that helped her overcome her handicap?

By the time they had gotten the door open to confirm what they were suspecting, her figure was already disappearing into the emptiness of the open highway, diminishing until completely lost in the most private of dreams.

He went to see Amarena the next day. He told the story, talking at great length. She listened raptly, not moving, expressionless. But at the end he caught a tear grooving her impassive face.

They gazed at one another for a long time. She said nothing. Neither did he. She pulled the pacifier from his mouth and put it on the night table. She took off her nightgown, standing there with her arms down, inviting him to admire her, her immaculate beauty. He gazed at her. She said nothing. Neither did he. His knees shook. Come, she said, finally. Drawing him by the wrist. He, frozen where he was. Come. But he was unable to move, much as he wanted to. She let his hand drop. She began to unbutton his shirt until it fell over his shoulders. He trembling wildly, the soft hands lowering his trousers, and the sweat blinding him, the hand brushing his testicles.

He shouted no, begged pardon, shouted no again, and begging pardon, he couldn't, no, her lips on his penis. He shut his eyes, his mind full of something that was nothing. Those men feathering him. No. He bit his lips. No. She told him to lie on the bed, drying the perspiration on his forehead with a silk handkerchief.

Why, Amarena?

He thought of those moist and tender lips when he saw the whores marching on Street of Visions led by two bands and a line of drum majorettes. Such a long time ago, yes, but it was unforgettable, unbearable. The people poking their heads out of the windows and applauding the demonstration. The people waving handkerchiefs. He saw the Chinese magician threading needles with his mouth while standing on one leg and regretted, yes, his behavior with Amarena. But she had understood, understood everything, then and always. She did not hold it against him. Rodri bought a big balloon which said in red letters on a white background SOUVENIR OF THE WHORES' STRIKE and in smaller letters Every penny a help. Thanks for your contribution. He had shouted that he couldn't, that he couldn't, and that soft hand slipping through his hair, the scented voice that calmed him, that it was alright, that it didn't matter.

Now, the whores demonstrating, children running after them pursued by fierce nuns with peaked hats trying to drive them home. The men came out of their shops to applaud and the rouge-smeared old ladies pretending to ignore it all. A crescendo of yelling and whistling paid tribute to the contingent of the Strip Teasers' Local waving little flags in the direction of their public and carrying a coffin covered with the inevitable black flowers and the inscription *Arriando el Bosque's Policy* to the hilarity of the crowd. Máximo thought that no, he had not been ruined forever, while before him the National Association of Pornographers and Perverts followed by a select collection of erotic dreams. He said goodbye to them as they passed, whistled a couple of times, and ended up applauding enthusiastically.

Why, Amarena?

She trying. He loved to feel that bedspread against his skin. She was smiling, he opened his eyes and was smiling, but no. Fearing that she would hate him, he needed her. You're just plain deflated, she said to him. Yes, I am. And, what a relief, she began to giggle, almost falling off the bed. You're incredible. Amarena. She put her hand over his mouth. I know. His eyebrows arched asking an explanation. She laughed, said that she remembered. Remembered what, he had asked. Dummy. Now they laughed together, holding hands. She leaned over the table to light a cigarette. What do you remember? Everything, everything.

Shit. It's that. The thing with Karen. I don't want to, I can't.

As you wish. But you are a bunch of crap, you are. You're just wasting your time. Think of alternatives, man. If you're going to curl up every time something nasty happens to you, you're done for. If you don't want to fuck, just come out with it...

Okay. I don't want to.

That's it. No sweat. I don't want to, period. As an obligation the hell with it.

It's that you attract me so.

Watch out. Take it back or I'll wring your thing.

Better let me go on telling about Karen. I'll get it out of my system that way.

Okay. As long as that's the end of this broken record. Tell me, where did you say that they found her?

On that highway, a few miles further on. There was a left-hand curve going downhill. That's where she lost control. She skidded sideways, the rear tire apparently hit the shoulder and she bounced motorcycle and all clear across the road. She landed headfirst and that was it. The motorcycle fell on top of her, skidded together with her into some rocks. So, you can imagine what the body looked like.

Amarena blew out some smoke as she drummed playfully on his belly. Okay, she said. She put out the cigarette in the ashtray. Another time, then. She leaned over to kiss him.

Three goddam years. Two since she's dead.

The demonstrators disappeared around a mysterious corner. The public faded away behind their doors. Nothing remained but the narrow empty street stained with sighs. Another time. But so far nothing.

Rodri and Máximo began walking back in the opposite direction from where the parade had disappeared. A vulture or two floated in the sky.

Jeezus! are they really going to get back on the roster? What a fucked-up world.

You forget what country we're in. They'll shoot 'em first.

Balls? The generals wouldn't dare... The Archbishop maybe...

They've done worse things.

I know, but never against whores.

That's true, but...

Now you're going to lay on the philosophy, there's always a first time, or something of the kind. Let's drop it and go kick a few.

My feet hurt.

Tomorrow then. How's the literature business doing?

Slow. But I managed to stay awake until half past three the other night.

Fantastic? It's a cinch you got a flair for that stuff.

They arrived, Máximo's house, and the street lights went on. The smell of refried beans penetrated through the front door. About to go in, Máximo remembered.

I'm getting together with Chingolo at The Last Goodbye tonight. Want to join us?

Jeeźus! But why the hell not? I wouldn't pass up a chance to kid the shit out of him about his nose.

Bring Pacha along. And don't go picking on Chingolo.

Me? Pick? When?

Rodri running off, pretending to chase a soccer ball. He leaped into the air, spun around, winked at Máximo and ran on.

That night, two drinks and Rodri was kidding the shit out of Chingolo about his nose. Pacha celebrating every sally, drumming on the table, and Máximo yelling *olé*, careful not to lose his pacifier. Chingolo squirming in his seat apologizing for its huge dimensions and form, a tragic existential situation, he said. But they did not stop bugging him. They kept on. And he laughing, giving it back to them.

Would it be possible to construct a universal system of ideas, like a map?

Jeezus! Hear what comes out of the man!

It is my opinion that organs of that nature must be of greater interest to us than the particular peculiarities of noses.

But your nose is an organ of that nature and almost a universal system in view of its size.

This perverse interest in my private parts. Scatological.

Olé.

Tell where you got it from, come on, man, tell.

When I was a very small boy. My parents had the custom of going out every night. They loved dancing, visiting friends. They were members of the International Oligarchs' Club. We had money. My father and mother were young and all that. They weren't happy unless they had people around them. Good man of action that my old man was, the process of thinking was dialectically merged with action. He organized really wild parties. The best pianists played in our living room. We never lacked the wherewithal. The joy of life was in action, and for him action meant dancing. They had a special nursemaid to look after me. A young Indian girl, very beautiful. Alsita. She knew only a little Spanish, the fragrances of all the flowers, and sang old songs. I attributed to her the many spiritual perfections that her voice and her face manifested but which she undoubtedly did not possess. Had I been her age, no doubt she would have been the kind of woman I would have been ready to die for but not live with, as Byron said. But I was only a little baby and she was my nursemaid. My parents went out every single night. And in three shakes of a lamb's tail, the nursemaid was in love. He was a very good-looking gardener with a thick mustache that drooped at the sides of his mouth. He worked at most of the houses in our neighborhood. Don Taco Umaña. He went barefooted and grew giant roses. But he was never able to see Alsita. She had to take care of me day and night. It's easy to win admiration when inaccessible but that wasn't enough for Alsita. She asked my mother if Don Taco could visit her from time to time. As a true Spanish lady my mother took offense. Her blood pressure dropped, she took to her bed suffering from *melancholia tremens*. She threatened to sack Alsita, to lower her wages, plenty low to begin with, to shoot Don Taco. Alsita withdrew her request. A few nights later, my mother, although still very pale, had recovered sufficiently to accompany my father to the monthly meeting of the Oligarchs' Club. Alsita was putting me to bed rather late when the dogs started barking. They barked furiously, noises, shouts, somebody could be heard desperately crying out. Alsita recognized the voice. She ran out with me in her arms, slamming doors, breaking a lamp. Don Taco had been trying to get in to see her. The dogs caught him in the middle of the garden. She ran at them shouting their names. He was on the ground, his arm caught in a dog's jaws, you could see the blood. She stepped into the middle of the fracas just as the dog snapped at his head. All he caught was my nose.

What happened then?

She fainted.

Be serious.

Seriously. They took me to the hospital. The other servants came out to separate the dogs and the people.

What happened to Don Taco and Alsita?

They ended up in the clink. My parents paid off the chief of police to kill them. They tied them to two poles in the form of an X and beat them with branches of thorns. After that they flayed off their skin and the chief of police put on Don Taco's and danced around the police station courtyard while the deputies shouted and clapped their hands. They sent the heads, hands, and feet to my parents who kept them on display in a bullet-proof glass case where they showed them off with pride for many years. Don Taco's head later won a blue ribbon in a taxidermy competition.

How did you know?

The family was proud of what they did. They told the story all the time.

Máximo suddenly yelled.

You're an older person, of course? Why didn't I think of it before? Tell me what it was like before the bombs. All that stuff happened before, didn't it?

Ay, the personal questions never end. Universal questions are ignored. Didn't you say that your father was a government employee before the bombs?

It seems so.

Don't worry. That happened before, but way before. In Ubico's time.

Who the fuck was Ubico?

Things of that sort were everyday occurrences in his day. Before the revolution.

Revolution? Listen to the guy!

Seriously. Ubico was a dictator and he was ousted by the revolution.

What's this wild stuff you're talking, man?

Jeezus! The guy is pissed.

There was a revolution? In this country? When?

Don't believe him, man. It's the booze talking.

There was. I'm serious. A revolution to get rid of the generals and monopolies and to reopen the university.

Impossible? How many drinks did you say you had?

The thing is that it's forbidden to mention it. Since the bombs. So, if you didn't lived through it...

Shall we order him a large black coffee?

Better yet, tea, no sugar, plenty of lemon.

Shitty bunch of skeptics. Listen. Let me tell you about it. Let me feed you a teaspoonful of reality to clear up your world view. Ignore my hiccups. There was a revolution at the beginning of the century to throw out the worst (hic) dictatorship the world has ever known. The people swarmed through every street shouting odes to (hic) freedom and killing the wives and children of the oligarchs. Happiness was the order of the day and there was food (hic) for all. But then the generals betrayed the people and went over to the side (hic) of the oligarchs. The new civilian government was defeated, the oligarchs gained absolute power with the help of their new (hic) allies and burned all their enemies. Every open space in the city blazed with human torches. The main square. The crazies' park. The Park of Discord. *El Carmen*. The Calvary (hic), of course. People were being burned alive everywhere while the oligarchs rode through the streets in carriages in their Sunday clothes. And things remained that way for a long time. Those were the days (hic) of Ubico. The *generalito* drove his Harley-Davidson up and down the city running people over. I was born towards the end of his career. Unhappiness had spread like the plague, there was misery everywhere, and so one day the people took to the streets (hic) to cleanse the country once again.

When?

1944.

Really?

I swear by my nose.

1944. Máximo deposited the date in his memory bank. Something had taken place in 1944 if this guy wasn't trying to kid him. A revolution. The generals and the monopolies were thrown out of the country and the university reopened. But with this guy you never know. He might have made it all up. But if he didn't, then people like his father had taken over the government and the sun came out. The plantations were confiscated and the land redistributed to those who needed it. Classes were held, books were being read, words were no longer illegal. It sounded like a dream, a fantasy. Maybe it was. That those times had really existed when no heads rolled and people were happy. When people like his father ruled the country. Could it be true?

And words were not illegal.

But then something happened. Something gave way. And the bombs began falling. And by the time he was finally able to come out all of that had been wiped out. The generals were back. Church bells filled the air. There were bonfires of books in all the parks. People like his father had disappeared. They were gone. Never to return?

All the pieces were beginning to fall into place.

Such a world had existed once in his own country, his own city. What a pity, he thought, what a pity that couldn't be more than the echo of a forgotten dream. What a pity, indeed. But his imagination was getting keener, he felt he was progressing. The words began coming out of him, slowly, painfully, one by one. He had to reconstruct that forgotten world even if it was only with words. To communicate the big lie that everything had been after the bombs. To keep that glorious past alive and vigorous. He would carve the words with his mind, put them together with great care until the concepts began to form, slowly, the concept of that world he had lost. To return words to the people, to fill in the blank spaces, the blanks.

He raced out of the cantina, ran the length of the whole city, ran towards home, down empty avenues where the street lamps like flaming bayonets held back the darkness. He ran, ran, ran, for blocks, many long blocks, a long time, on the way to his mother.

Mother? Tell me about 1944! Tell me about 1944!

She trembled. Just on hearing that year, that date. She'd been hiding it. Without batting an eye she asked him where he had heard it, where it came from. He said that he had rediscovered the secret faces of those who now, after the bombs, were condemned to oblivion.

She motioned to him to sit down beside her and he did. That he should pay close attention and he did. But before beginning her story, she talked to him about what a bad thing it was to masturbate.

Máximo did not sleep all that night.

CHAPTER 6

DAWN

A new U.S. ambassador arrived soon after Karen's father's replacement had been recalled to Washington. The coup he had engineered did not have the effectiveness expected of career diplomats. Arriando el Bosque was caught redhanded. They had to send him to the Vatican as military attaché. A new general appeared to keep an eye on the civilian government. Order was re-established. The people were all smiles again.

Máximo.

Yes.

Sit here. Next to me. You're very far away.

The day the guerrillas killed the new ambassador, Máximo ran to Amarena's house. Word began to spread. Washington demanded vengeance. The ships could be seen coming expressionlessly into sight where sky and sea meet. A new team of technical advisers was expected at any moment. The army was on full alert. But, fortunately, the government had someone to blame. Word began to spread in the city, rapidly, throughout the city. Surprise, anger, and consternation among the people. The government had decided that the whores were responsible.

Did she know? Máximo spotted an empty can in the middle of the street. He kicked it hard trying to score in the mouth of a sewer. He missed by inches. The can hit the edge of the sidewalk and bounced away the entire length of the street scattering glass shards on all sides. Did she know?

She knew. Strangers were not allowed into the house. The Señorita was not in. The Señorita was not in. But for him she was in. Máximo saw the pistol butt sticking out of the butler's pocket. He was led smilingly to the familiar room.

I have nothing to be afraid of, Máximo. After all, I'm am American citizen. As a matter of fact the CIA just phoned. They are sending two marines to guard the door. Isn't that wild? I hope they're cute. But, seriously. It's the others that worry me. I hid some at the Union Church, but there's so many of them.

It was on the front pages the next day. To everyone's relief, only the seven strike leaders were being accused of the assassination. There were twelve to start with. But Amarena had managed to spirit four of them out of the country disguised as a team of bridge players en route to a tournament. The government will not tolerate blackmail, the newspaper said. The government will not tolerate social disruption. The seven women captured the previous day were tried at midnight in the Santa Teresa dungeons and sentenced before dawn. Washington, ecstatic. A cable from the State Department already, welcoming the quick response of the democratic government. The execution was scheduled for 4 p.m. In the National Stadium. The public cordially invited to attend.

I'm delighted to have you looking at me, Máximo, but I can't allow myself the luxury of catching another cold.

Amarena insisting she had to go. And along with Chingolo, who was not there, Máximo was trying to convince her that it would be best not to. She had taken several Valiums with a glass of water, she said. It was her duty to attend. Máximo arguing strongly against it. She began to whimper and yell, threaten to, insulting him, threatening never to speak to him again. He gave in. She sent him to order the car.

How can they do it, Máximo? How?

He trying not to laugh. Typical Protestant conscience, no? This is Latin America, no? She had lived in the country for some time, no? She was accustomed to its ways by now, no? And that Washington was going to grant the generals another loan as a reward, no?

But picking on the whores is the limit.

That's how it goes.

By one in the afternoon the lines at the stadium were already interminable. Thermos bottles and lunch boxes stretched for blocks and blocks from the Avenue of Athletes, under the railroad bridge, passing along the Alley of the Lame, The Avenue of Misfortune, the Boulevard of Hairy-Chested Machos, the Alley of the Dispossessed, Ground Corn Square, and Cat Piss Lane, as far as Station Avenue, climbing to Barrios Square, and ending at the Calvary Church steps where the acolytes were selling incense and *tostadas* with beans. Shifty characters hung around the gates offering fistfuls of bills for a ticket. Peddlers running up and down the the long lines hawking oranges, oranges with salt and chili, fruit drinks of all flavors, pineapple and tamarind, sweet rolls, sacks of potato chips, peanuts at 5 centavos a bag, salted popcorn. Bottles were not allowed into the stadium for fear that some overwrought fan might throw one at the field and seriously injure a presidential candidate. Everybody was frisked before entering. Everybody was buying sun visors because of the glare. Red ones, and green and blue, too, lots of sun visors, and some wore palm leaf hats and dark glasses. Policemen and soldiers with machine guns in evidence everywhere, guardians of order, smiling, to ensure the peaceful course of the event. Curious vultures perched on the crests of the cypress trees around the stadium. It was a sad occasion.

Rah, rah, rah, sis boom bah! Alaveevo, alavaivo, alaveevo, veyevo, voo! The whores, the whores, they'll come through!

Máximo and Amarena seated in a box. A huge woodpile had been burned in the center of the field. When the stadium gates were opened, workers with long poles were still spreading the embers. To form a ring of fire. A big urn at each corner of the stadium with burning incense. They dragged an enormous stone block to the center of the field. Máximo told her they could still leave. She asked for orange juice.

The national anthem. Everybody stood. An endless line of fat generals and pink-cheeked men with top hats began to fill the stand of honor. The audience whistling at them. The civilian president smiled wanly at the acting ambassador. Gunshots put a stop to the whistling.

After some five minutes the seven victims came onto the field through the Triumphal Arch. The public rose to applaud them, to keep their spirits up. Some even set off fireworks even though they were forbidden on this occasion, sky rockets bursting mischievously in the air. There were shouts of "Death to the army goons!" Amarena applauded in response and Máximo scratched the tip of his nose. The victims walked barefooted, wearing white robes reaching down to their ankles, hands tied behind their backs. Two guards in freshly laundered uniforms escorted each prisoner to the center of the field. A chorus of "Untie their hands, untie their hands" from the south stands. But the sound of gunshots was immediately followed by silence. The sun just on the point of being hidden by a bank of clouds coming from the north.

The chief executioner emerged with his four assistants through a small door at one side. All wore long black robes with hoods over their heads and a white cross on the chest. The light-hearted Archbishop ran to the center of the field to shake hands with the executioners who knelt before him. The Archbishop took the opportunity to kiss them on the forehead, whispering something to each, and then turned to bless the victims. All refused to kneel. The Archbishop frowned and Amarena applauded. Máximo looked all around to see whether any policeman had noticed. The fourth victim spat in the Archbishop's face. The whole stadium applauded. The Archbishop burst into tears and said to her you nasty thing, you, then condemned her to eternal damnation as the sexton wiped off the holy countenance.

The sentences were read out to the accompaniment of generalized whistling. The acting ambassador formally accepted the execution as retribution for the crime against his country. The Defense Minister rose to announce that from this day on a strike of any nature would be punishable by death. Curfew was moved back to 8 o'clock.

The first victim was brought forward. One of her guards untied her and the other removed the robe. She was dark-skinned, cinnamon color, short, heavy legs, breasts a pair of pendulums. The Archbishop buried his face in the sexton's chest. Two of the assistant executioners took her by the hands and forced her to sit on the cold stone block. The other two quickly seized her ankles. All pulled at the same time. She remained lying on the stone struggling to keep her head up. She had long black hair and her mouth was open. The chief executioner holding smoking incense burners over her, and after taking a last swig of *Indita*, he tipped the bottle to drip over the victim's body. He took out the long obsidian knife. She shook her head violently, her eyes enormous. The chief executioner bent over her and with a flick of the wrist jabbed the knife in under her ribs. The body arched in a final convulsion. The chief executioner plunged his hand into the body and tore out the still beating heart, lifting it over his head, offering it to the guests of honor as he shouted *"Dios, Patria y Libertad."* He was covered with blood. His face completely red. His clothes. Dripping red, red on black, over the white cross, all red. The stadium was screaming, screaming in a collective shriek of being and hatred, impotent, looking on, doing nothing but looking, unable to act. Never again. The other victims were trying to see without seeing. Two of the guards pissed in their pants. Obscenities could be heard from every direction. One woman tore her hair out. Others shook their fists. Amarena hid her face in Máximo's quivering chest, as he muttered "*Adiós, Patria y Libertad.*"

The body was dumped in a corner of the stadium. The second victim was brought forward, the vultures wheeling over the stands, the sky completely black. The second victim fought wildly with the guards, cursed them, kicked them. The guards slapped her in the face, she dropped to the ground and refused to move. One of the guards began kicking her between the legs. A spectator jumped over the barbed wire fence to go to her aid. A single burst of machine gun fire was heard and the spectator fell as though electrocuted by lightning. Silence reigned. They pulled her by the hair to the block as she fought desperately to the last. Amarena shouted, let's get out of this shit, jumping to her feet, fulminating against the guests of honor with her eyes of fire and vengeance, rancor and madness, and hate, hate, hate.

The streets were enveloped in total silence. The first raindrops began to fall. Amarena was hardly able to walk. Máximo half carried, half dragged her, weeping, trembling, I hate them, shouted Amarena, I hate them. She vomited in front of the car, he holding her up around the waist. Not so tight, she told him. Not so tight.

And she spent the next three nights struggling to wipe away the nightmares with heavy doses of

Valium. Máximo went to the house every afternoon and the butler let him know how she was doing. Finally, she was able to receive him on the fourth day.

The usual mischievous sparkle was back in her eyes. But he also found her staring blankly into space from time to time. Deep circles under her eyes. Laughing sensually, nonetheless. Lips fresh. He sat down on the edge of the bed.

You're looking fine.

Liar.

They laughed. He recounted some tidbits of political gossip. She responded well. She had recovered better than he expected. Then why not tell her now what he hadn't been able to yet? He could hardly wait. Here goes.

I have something to tell you.

She froze in the middle of his sentence, catching the urgency of his tone. He was surprised at her reaction. She melted him with a smile.

Tell.

I know everything at last. My mother isn't toothless. It's just that her teeth are transparent.

What do you mean? She told you?

And how! You should have seen her, Amarena! Once she let herself go it was as though she had no substance, no image, as though she were nothing but the incarnation of the words themselves, sounds coming from between a pair of floating lips.

Máximo pacing back and forth, carried away, hands behind his back, chin sunk on his chest. Listen to me, son, she said, and listen closely because you may never hear these words again. And I could feel the allergy coming out on my face and remember the smell of the rotting corpses. Because her voice was timeless and in listening I lived and relived in my own flesh those long, lost years. Listen to me, son, and I sat down with my eyes closed so that I could see her words. And she told me about my father, too, and in talking to me about him she talked about me, about always, about the world, about life. Everything fell into place, Amarena. My father, the bombs, even that story the old man once told me. Because everything began at the beginning, Amarena, at our beginning. With Don Tecún. His death in Pacajá was pretty much our death and the bodies I remember seeing were the rotting bodies on the plains of Xelajú. And since that year 1520 until today we keep on killing only the horse. And the quetzales will not sing any longer and our cities will go on burning. He was right, Amarena. The old man was right. His story told me where my father was. Who he was. A truth isn't always a truth you can see and can touch. But remember. It's a truth, anyway, as great if not greater, than any other truth.

I think you've lost me now.

My mother told me the story, another story and the same story. How she saw the country burning from end to end, the charred bodies thrown like garbage into mass graves. How bravely they fought to bring it out of the darkness in '44. She met my father fighting in the streets. And then your Thunderbolts buried her in '54. Only ten years of light. It's the lack of warmth that makes the earth heal so slowly.

Máximo. They weren't *my* Thunderbolts.

Excuse me. I meant to say...

Alright, it's okay. Go on.

It began in June, 1944, when the mountains and fields are greenest. The dogs howled all night. All night, son, I couldn't sleep well and woke up with a headache. But the big toe on my left foot was hurting and that always meant a special day, and so I tried to ignore it. A big demonstration was scheduled for that day, Amarena. I was just out of high school and full of illusions, son, and we had decided to go, my brothers and sister, cousins, and all our friends. And my mother, your grandmother, in an absolute panic, worrying about what might happen to us. What if things get out of control? But we insisted. And so they all went to the demonstration, Amarena, lining up around midday for the long march. All of them dressed in black. It was Ubico's fourteenth year in power, Amarena. And we walked, son, taking care not to step in the sewage that ran down all the streets, and with clothespins on our noses. My mother, your grandmother, had decided that the soldiers' boots would be untied and that they would trip but I knew that in case of danger our own feet could get stuck in the mud. We kept together, son, for fear that Ubico would come around a corner on his Harley-Davidson and run us down. He always rode counter-clockwise and with a pair of binoculars hanging from around his neck, all the better to see you with. And if he saw us? It was every citizen's duty, set forth in the constitution, to let himself be run over by him. After all, he was the president. And the incidence of street crime had decreased during his reign. What to do if he appeared with those sunglasses you could see your own reflection in, and that smell of burning rubber? Of course, there were some who defended his regime. There was order, things were under control, the streets were safe. Parades were long and colorful, watches and calendars were forbidden. But the bad smell finally penetrated everything, those open sewers, and finally everybody was out on the street. We didn't know what time it was but we knew that the time had come. We were just waiting for a sign, son. My mother, your grandmother, had told us over and over again how the earthquake of '17 had roused the people to throw out Cabrera. She often told the story in the secrecy of the night. Citizens feared Ubico's long ears, all the better to hear you with. About the time the last adobe had fallen with a great crash, the whole town had unearthed their carbines and were on their way to La Palma, Cabrera's headquarters. And it took only one week of bloody fighting to overthrow the 22-year-old regime. So we waited for a sign, son. And then in June of '44 it began raining ashes. The volcano had been peaceful for a long time. We all ran to brush off the carbines hidden among the spider webs. My younger brother ran to the corner store to buy oil. There was a guest in the house at the time, an American, a friend of one of my brothers who was working in the Canal Zone. He went paler and paler as our energy mounted. My mother, your grandmother, cleaned the dust off her prayer book.

The demonstration was at midday, Amarena, when the sun is strong enough to blind you. Since it was the first demonstration of the season, it was planned as a peaceful one. The carbines had been left at home. The women marched at the head, son, because the soldiers had never shot at us before. We carried beautiful placards calling for Ubico's resignation, and we laughed a lot.

She remembered that afternoon clearly, Amarena. The machine guns opened fire as they were passing the Street of Bitterness. She saw her fall. María Chinchilla. A teacher. We have a symbol, someone shouted. And everybody felt sure that this was it. I had been standing beside her only a moment before, son, and now she was stretched out on the sidewalk. All the zenzontles flew into the trees of the main square and began a long, shrill lament. And my mother went running down the Street of Bitterness daring the soldiers to shoot her, Amarena, unconsciously repeating to herself that one and one are two times sixteen makes thirty-two. Afraid of tearing her stockings, Amarena.

And the soldiers charged again, faces expressionless. And one of them had picked me out and was turning his rifle on me, son, when a man with a great big handlebar mustache came out of nowhere, picked me up and threw himself with me in his arms behind a parked car. My father, Amarena. My father. And the bullet smashed the back window. With an intimate laugh he kissed her hand, whispering his name, at your service. There we were, watching the tear gas bombs exploding, son, over us on all sides and fortunately my stockings held out.

Together we looked at the wet garbage all over the street, son, the bushes and dead trees. And when the bullets had finally set the car that was our shelter on fire, we managed to escape in the confusion and black smoke toward the Avenue of Faith, but a stray bullet grazed his hip and he fell into the filth of an open sewer. She saw her savior fall, Amarena, and ran to the drug store across the street for an inexpensive cologne to pour over him to kill the stench, son, and then I helped him get up, and we went staggering home between the puddles of the Street of Sighs. The shooting could still be heard when we knocked on the door and my mother, your grandmother, opened it with tears in her eyes. My old cat had died.

And Ubico decided that it was time to take a holiday to San Francisco and he went there on a scholarship from the Fruit Company, leaving General Ponce Vaides in the hot seat. The last hundred days of darkness had begun. Everyone came together in the darkness to wait for the dawn. But it was cold, son, and even though the people were impatient and ready, I was afraid that the darkness and the cold would defeat them at the last minute. What if the dawn never came? What if the night refused to disappear? I was afraid. Was my family asleep, too? But then I heard the rumbling of the toilet. I laughed. That dispelled my fear. My younger brother at least was awake. And then my mother's false teeth. She was cold, yes, but she was ready, too. Like me. She sent me to look for white corn and yellow corn.

And my mother went to Ciro's, Amarena. Everybody went to Ciro's in those days, son, the men all wearing jackets and neckties. It was the city's most popular night club. But that evening the men all wore jeans and windbreakers and I couldn't understand why they let them in. A friend saw me and told me to go right home, son. I tried to detect if he had alcohol on his breath. Nothing but ice water that night, he told me. Then why leave? He just smiled. Others came by and said the same thing. And so I left very excited and on stepping outdoors I saw the morning star in the middle of the sky.

When my mother was just two blocks from home a single cannon went off. The burst arched gracefully across the sky like a comet with a tail of a thousand colors, son, above the entire city that hadn't slept that night. And with the sun peeking over the horizon, it fell like a shooting star from the sky straight into the munitions depot at San José. The fort was blown sky high and the world began to move.

My mother was waiting for me at the front door. Mom, the revolution! Yes, yes, get into the house quickly, she said, and the clattering of the machine guns had already begun. Our American guest, his face white, hands trembling, was pacing the hall. I couldn't help laughing and his eyes filled with tears. Please take me to the airport! For God's sake take me to the airport! We can't, she said happily. We can't, I said, beaming with happiness, we can't, the planes aren't going anywhere today, she said to him, we can't, we can't, and I shut my eyes, we can't because the revolution has begun, and I sat down in the patio to watch the flowers blossom.

And the sun rose with the explosions in the sky. The little animals, and the big animals were overjoyed in the rivers, the ravines, the mountain peaks. Everybody looked towards the sun. The mountain lion and the jaguar roared. The quetzal rose into the air, tracing elegant circles with his green-feathered tail, and he began to sing and the eagle spread its wings, ready to depart. And the swampy surface of the earth began to dry and there was solid ground on which to stand. And all the generals and colonels turned to stone. I was in the middle of the patio watching, son, thinking of everything my dead cat had missed. There was a candle in my hand, and she said in a loud voice, I have seen the sun, and she blew out the candle and gazed at the column of smoke dispersing into the soft, cool air and the last drop of wax solidifying on her brown skin.

Her younger brother then came out. He was in his third year of college but classes had been cancelled that year. I'm going he said. And I asked him where, son. To fight. He had the family carbine that glittered in the sunlight. The same one, Amarena, that my grandfather had taken into the streets in 1920. The same one that my great-grandfather had marched on the city with in 1871. And when my mother saw him she ran to the kitchen to grind the yellow corn and the white corn to make *atole* for everyone to drink. The mice all lined up and stood at attention in the entranceway as he walked out.

The students had taken to the streets. There were long lines at the Honor Guard headquarters, tall men and short, rich men and barefooted men, all waiting for a rifle and a handful of rusty bullets. To the streets. On Reforma Avenue. All the way down to Avenue of Miracles and Street of Hope. Passing La Palma, crossing by the train station and the telegraph office. Along Barrios Square to the main square.

The government was preparing its exodus. The remains of San José were still smouldering, the generals already running towards the national treasury to get money for the long trip. Sweaty and unshaven, shoes unlaced, neckties askew, they ran with their duffle bags while tense, downcast lieutenants dickered with the revolutionary leaders for safe-conducts to the airport where the plane was already warming up. Time to go.

Policemen struggled to get out of uniform before a bullet found them. They scattered through the deserted streets in shorts and socks trying to find a hole in which to bury their heads.

And on that golden afternoon of October 20, the last cannon shot was heard from Fort Matamoros. After that, silence. Arana, Toriello, and Arbenz, the leaders of the revolution, were already on their way to the National Palace. Groups of students ran through the streets announcing to the populace that the twentieth century had finally arrived.

Very soon there wasn't a soldier or policeman left. The last one was seen at four in the afternoon on kilometer 23.5 of the Honduras highway, his skin black and blue, his sky-blue shorts with yellowish stains. A long whistle was heard. The Boy Scouts in short pants marching in formation to take charge of directing traffic. And on every street a student patrol with red armbands and one weapon. Stay home! Everybody stay home! Stray bullets are flying around. Stay in your houses! But people were fighting to come out on the street, ringing neighbors' door bells to hug and kiss. The finest wines and fanciest glasses were brought out. Drinks, drinks for all. The old folks carried their chairs to the sidewalk to gaze up at the cloudless sky. The shy little old man who lived on the corner of Street of Sighs trotted out a marimba. The avenue was closed to traffic and the instrument was soon ringing out a Guatemalan *son*. Fireworks were set off on the street corners, sky rockets and Roman candles of the most expensive type, burst after giddy burst, sending shivers up the Boy Scouts' backs. Toothless old men in bathrobes and slippers claiming to have marched with Barrios in 1871 shot off their old carbines and danced with their fat spouses. A Red Cross ambulance parked around the corner and two nurses in white uniforms sat on the edge of the sidewalk waiting. One of them yawned. A little girl in a yellow cotton dress approached them timidly. Her mother said that there were one drunk and two corpses in the shop on the corner and what should she do with them because they were blocking the entrance. Across the street a white-haired man was opening a bottle of champagne and the church bells were overwhelmed by the explosive notes of the marimba that blotted out everything else. Many ladies and slim gentlemen smelling of gunpowder began to dance, one, two, turn, one, two, turn. The aroma of victory. Three blocks away the students were piling up the uniforms of the policemen and soldiers, shields, cartridge belts, officers' caps, truncheons, a boot without laces, a hand with three fingers, a pair of overshoes, an officers' manual, a small bottle of rum, a pair of motorcycling boots with the roasted feet inside and a bone sticking out. The pile was set on fire and the people ran to sit around the blaze, the kids bringing chairs for the old folks with arthritis and everybody singing songs of loneliness and love and taking turns leading chants.

A student was seen galloping along the avenue on a white horse and when he reached the bonfire he flew over the flames in a great leap applauded by all. Rumors followed in his wake. Somebody said that he was a distant relative. The student greeted them and gave the good news. Long was leaving. The people went into shock. They chorused his words trying to believe them. Ambassador Long was leaving. A great shout rose from every throat higher than the column of smoke, provoking two heart attacks and one coughing fit. The grandchildren picked up the chairs and the crowd headed towards Airport Avenue. Two men who lived next to the Capuchin Church offered to give anybody unable to run a ride in their wagon. The marimba was covered to protect it from the dampness of the night.

They arrived in time to see a long limousine approaching. The avenue was lined with ecstatic people stretching as far as the empty terminal hidden by the cypress trees. The tail of the plane with hateful red and black stripes could be seen behind the wall. Two men with revolutionary armbands cleared the way on motorcycles, requesting the people not to throw fruits or vegetables.

> Bye, bye, Boaz Long!
> At last you go home!
> Bye, bye Boaz Long!
> At last you go home!

And they threw rotten fruits and vegetables as the old man passed by, the swollen, pink old man with the top hat, who on orders from his government, had tried to keep the dawn from breaking.

As he was driven towards the waiting plane, firemen played "Las Golondrinas" for him on trumpets and the people waved handkerchiefs. A short, fat man began to sing it. "Goodbye, lovely Mariquita," terribly out of tune. The people didn't budge from where they stood when they saw the propellors begin to turn over clockwise one after the other and the plane move slowly to the head of the runway. Nobody moved, nobody spoke. The plane swung its nose in the direction of Volcano Agua and an old woman laughed, the motors roaring, the brakes released at last, all eyes helping the machine elevate and gain altitude and remaining fixed upon it as it flew south over Amatitlán, banked, gaining more altitude over the volcano, and everybody laughed, and yet higher, until it melted into the full moon peeping over the horizon.

Bye, bye Boaz Long!
At last you go home!

Night fell and the people were still dancing and the rumors still flying, as the Red Cross searched for bodies and the Boy Scouts, trembling with cold, picked their noses. Then the great rumor began to circulate. Arévalo's coming. Arévalo's coming, everybody was saying, Arévalo's coming. Did you hear? Arévalo's already on his way! Arévalo? Arévalo! Coming? Arévalo's already on his way. He left Buenos Aires just this morning, Arévalo, and after missing the 8:40 train, he had been seen astride a big, strong mule, making his way across the Chaco. The condors were waiting there to guide him across the Andes. The llamas were on general alert. Money was rolling in the streets. How long would Arévalo take to get here? Three days to cross the Andes? And the Amazon jungle, what about that? Would he stop off for hats in Ecuador, swim across the Canal right under the noses of the dozing planes? How long will he take? Would he skip over Costa Rica and skirt the great Nicaraguan lakes? When would he arrive?

And my mother, your grandmother, and I lifted the huge crock of *atole* and put it on the goat cart, son, and went out in the street. It was a huge clay crock your great-grandmother had made to celebrate Barrios' arrival in 1871. It was some job moving it, the streets were still muddy and the wheels were getting stuck all the time. We would stop to offer a cup of *atole* to the Boy Scouts with their short pants and rabbity eyes who were discharging their revolutionary duties on every corner. And we went the whole length of Gaiety Avenue, son, from north to south, as far as the station and then along Avenue of Love, me with my eyes peeled for my younger brother who was nowhere to be seen. Where could that kid have gone? We weren't about to check the lists of the dead. We knew he was alive. And then southward on Avenue of Desire, the crock three-quarters empty. I started to feel chilly, my shawl wasn't exactly new. But we continued on our way back down Avenue of Hope, with no more than a few spoonfuls of *atole* still left and one of the wheels about ready to drop off. There was no *atole* for the students who had occupied police headquarters, so we just smiled at them, thinking we'd be back. Then we heard a whistle. Mom? Yes? A whistle. Yes. And again. There it is again, Mom! We stopped and looked in all directions. It was the family whistle, no question about it. The goat sneezed. It's coming from over our heads. Yes. We looked up, above the Spanish moss on the walls, above the dried blood and the crumbling bricks. Further up, still further, up to the highest part of the tower. A pair of eyes was whistling proudly at us. The guard! Mom, the guard! It was her younger brother, Amarena, who was up there.

Máximo.

Yes?

Sit here. Next to me. You're too far away.

She took off her nightgown and remained sitting there in the middle of the bed, allowing him all the time he wanted to look at her. He sucked on his teeth, noted the slight dip in her breasts hiding the bones of her chest. More than anything he liked her legs.

I love having you look at me Máximo but I can't allow myself the luxury of catching another cold.

Máximo smiled timidly, lowering his gaze a little. He tucked his pacifier away in his shirt pocket.

Chingolo was telling me the other day that...

A man with a Roman nose. Remember this. Never trust a man with a Roman nose even if he has the smoothest complexion in the world. Take off your clothes and come up here, okay?

Her laugh dissolved into a kiss. He was hesitant. She crawled toward him. Helping him with his trousers that clung to his legs, the perspiration. And in just a moment he was stretched out beside her. She slipped her arms under his shoulders and brought him close. Stretched out in bed, both heads resting on the satin pillows.

My father was short and timid, Amarena. Like me. He easily caught cold and allergies. He had a hoarse voice and no ear for music. He was good-looking but lacked a strong personality. Scrupulously honest. His greatest fear was of ending up an alcoholic with a three-day's growth of beard staggering down alleys shouting at kids trying to play soccer.

Máximo engulfed in those bottomless eyes, angry with boredom.

Women felt at ease with him. He instilled confidence, the perfect gentleman. People could tell him all their problems any time of day and he felt for them and offered useless advice. And he never learned to dance. He would sit in his rattan chair in the patio to watch his belly bulge and pull hairs out of his chest. He was always afraid of losing his loved ones.

She told him he could rest his hands on the soft mass of her drowsing breasts.

He was very fond of soccer and dreaded poverty and want. He had no patience with generals and limousines. According to what they tell me, he was the kind of absolutely ordinary man never mentioned in songs or stories and rudely ignored by the champagne drinkers. And then one bright and sunny day he dug up a dust-covered gun and went out to join the revolution.

She felt his hand. Rubbing her belly, finally. Such a pleasant feeling. She closed her eyes.

He marched with the peasants and labor unions to rid the country of uniformed men. He served the revolution in the streets and then sat down without a complaint at a plain pine desk in a forgotten corner

164

of the National Palace, always so proud of his big mustache. Until the day the bombs caught him unawares behind a stack of papers of no importance.

He stopped moving. She opened her eyes.

It was all so simple. No problem. Your government pissed off at ours. And they had all the planes. Mr. Foster Sucks' ulcer flared up that morning and he telephoned Panama in a rage. The planes took off quietly from the Canal Zone, that chastity belt of Latin America, refueled in Nicaragua with Tacho Somoza's blessing, and flew over our territory in the afternoon. June 18th. The planes didn't even touch down. They dropped their infernal load and skipped in the darkness of night. The next morning they were back sunning themselves next to the Gatun Locks. It was in the Canal that they deflowered us and it's from the Canal that they keep fucking us.

Beads of perspiration came out on her forehead and between her breasts. She asked him what happened to his father.

My mother never heard of him again. She wouldn't admit it, either. She lived in hope that one day he would come back, that she would hear, that she would know. She refused to, couldn't, tell me that she didn't know either. She, living in a dream, he gone with the old dream of Arbenz, different reality. He could have died in the streets, gun in hand. He could have been taken prisoner and put up against an anonymous wall, his body disappeared into an unmarked grave. He could have escaped to Mexico like so many others. He could have died under the bombarded ruins of the revolution.

She felt a chill. She saw how pale he was. But he didn't try to stop her, finally, and she playing with him happily, pale but going on with his story.

I don't think he escaped, though. We would have heard about him. The Mexican authorities say they have no record of his name.

Her teeth biting his ear. He letting her, his hands slipping over her back, that back, gently.

He must be dead. He must have died in the street defending...

Come inside me.

He would have died before giving in to foreign domination. To die so that I could live. And now I can try to tell the story that everybody is trying to forget.

Her hips now rolling, she happy, yes. He pale but unresisting, letting himself be led, his hips rolling to the rhythm of his words, his fingers burying themselves in those brown buttocks.

I have to tell the story, Amarena. I have to tell it, word by word. My style is getting better every second.

I'm sure of it!

Her hair flying in all directions and her slender fingers now digging into his sweating thighs, still trying to understand that unceasing voice.

That night I finally managed to keep awake all night trying to find answers to the unanswerable questions. And every night since then.

Now their bodies drenched in sweat, her teeth making black and blue marks on his neck, fear and talk, talk, tongues without meeting, and that silken, skillful hand, enfolding his testicles.

Tomorrow, tomorrow, I'm buying a parrot. I'm coming along, Amarena, I'm coming along.

Me too, me too.

Embraced, the heat of their skin scorching one another, contraction upon contraction, shouts and words, nails scratching the trembling back, that wet ear in her mouth, legs tangled, buttocks tightening and straining, quivering.

I'll find my father through words. I'll bring him back to life with words. I will build a cathedral of words. I'll create a country with my words. In my words I'll find the universe and I'll understand the eternal present through my words. In my words, I will find, I will end, I will become the words themselves, become words, words, words, I will incarnate words, words, words.

Their eyes found each other again. Completely relaxed. She smiled. He as though discovering for the first time. What had happened to him? She, telling him not to move. He, almost passed out, telling her that he wanted to embrace her more, to hold her, press his face closer against hers. Smiles blooming.

Crazed Máximo.

They rested, caresses and whispering and little smiles, hands joined, feet reaching for feet, dreams finding one another.

I'm tired of corpses. I've seen so many. It wouldn't be all that bad if they smelled better. I refuse to live that smell again, I refuse.

Your poor nostrils.

My poor nostrils.

But you're growing up. And what an ordeal it was. Now, all you have to do is start taking action.

With everything. Against everything.

That's what I like to hear. None of that in one ear and out the other.

I'm doing good.

You're doing good. And you'll be doing even better.

What I want to do is say all the things that others keep back. Remind the people of those great years before the bombs, that past that they are forcing us to forget. To be able to feel all those blank pages that are collecting dust in our libraries. I detest these times. The dream of revolution was better. I want to bring back those times. With words.

It seems to me I heard that somewhere already about the past having been better.

No, man, this is different.

Sure, sure. And you're so funny you're going to make all the generals laugh.

I'll make them laugh. They'll laugh and laugh and laugh so hard that their bellies will swell up and burst.

Poor generals.

I will exaggerate. I will lie. Chingolo says that you must lie to be understood. It's another way of getting inside a person. If I begin lying fast and furious they'll begin to listen to me. Lies are sacred, Amarena.

Become a word, then. Or even a tin soldier, if you want. So long as you always make stopovers in my bed.

CHAPTER 7

THE SALAD
OF THE FLAMES

How's life treating you, Chingolito, tell me.

Compulsions, convulsions, repulsions, revulsions, *darlingcita*.

Coffee?

Black, black, no sugar. I am bitter, bitter.

And the boy prodigy?

Strutting about the park, now spouting words, now kicking goals.

He's growing up on us, eh?

Taking giant steps.

Is he on his way?

To a dungeon. Life's a western to him.

Maybe by a fluke.

You've already happened to him. Do you expect him to hit the lottery every day?

He's improving.

I haven't read over his fantasies lately.

Who's talking of words?

It was on the front pages the next morning. The country was coming closer and closer to civil war. Máximo knew that. The German Ambassador had been kidnapped. He knew that, too. The government declined to negotiate. A known fact. The German Ambassador had been executed. Inevitable. The new government of General "Spider" Arana had declared a war of extermination against the guerrillas. Just like all the previous governments. Curfew was in force. What else was to be expected? State of siege in place. Big surprise. The regime didn't even try to conceal its movements. The army, air force, all the secret police agencies were carrying out massive operations and making thousands of arrests. Máximo yawned. Complaints were continuing about the high levels of blood in the municipal water supply. Really? The government had begun importing potable water from Miami. And if that wasn't enough, there were the hippies. The hippies, the hippies, horrors, the hippies. Máximo folded the paper and threw it on the table. Nothing new that day.

He returned to his desk. Smiling, he sat down. A pile of yellow pages was growing next to his bed.

He was now staying awake nights and writing.

He had new things to worry about. Whether or not his characters were boring, his plots too involved. So many things to be thought out with the greatest of care. That he didn't have a sure enough grasp of language, that he shouldn't get messed up in sentimentality or arrogance. All those imaginary criticisms to face up to, to overcome. What the hell was he doing writing rubbish, anyway? He ought to go to the mountains and fight like a man. But his aim was no good and his pencils were sharpened. And he had bought himself a parrot. A green, medium-size parrot that perched on his left shoulder, scratched at the fleas under his wing, and screeched: *All against the wall!*

Many afternoons the words wouldn't sing. But his imagination was growing, too. He dreamed. It was growing big and sturdy like the carnations in the patio. Like the begonias.

He heard noise in the bushes. Yes. And scared to death. Flattened out on the ground. Footsteps crackling. Crackling. He saw the boots going by. First one. Crushing the dry twigs. And the green pants legs. He was sweating. Then the other one. Crackling. And the noise faded. They were safe. And just then the chattering. Machine guns. They were cooked. He turned to look at Rodri. His face was white, tears running down his cheeks. But he smiled. Hand steady on the rifle. Tight against his chest. He saw Pacha, too, flat on the ground. Little pebbles sticking to his cheeks. And the chattering guns. The chattering that didn't have the courage to stop. He laughed.

Words. The words were coming out.

Then the bursts that had lasted for hours and hours and hours and the helicopter that began circling overhead, circling. They stayed crouched down. And the smoke. The smoke into the nose, mouth, eyes. And it circled and circled. For hours. Rodri gnawing at his thumb and then the chattering again. And again. Shit. Not moving all day long, wait all day long for dark. Chattering and the helicopter circling, circling again and the smoke.

Who did they burn? Who did they rape? Who did they shoot at? Who did they beat? Who did they rob? Who did they bomb? Who did they kill? And the circling, circling, and the gunfire and the smoke. Shit.

Jesus, Mary, and Joseph! Are you going to eat or not? The beans are getting cold! And if you think I'm going to reheat them for you, you've got another think coming! Where do you come off, you lousy kid, shut up in your room all day long!

But in spite of everything he had gone to the Ministry of Culture to apply for an artist's certificate. I write. They stared at him in disbelief. That's illegal. Unless you are a diplomat. Even the snakes respect guerrillas like César Montes. That's what he told them. César Montes is illegal, too. Yon Sosa sleeps inside an alligator's belly to fool the soldiers. He told them that, too. Everything's illegal. But they took down everything. But didn't they say writing was prohibited? And they stared at him. What else? What else did he know? The spider monkeys help the guerrillas cross the Verapaces and the vultures warn them when planes are coming. That and more and then more. But the way things were he'd never make it, never get his artist's certificate. It couldn't be done. They refused. So, he'd have to be satisfied with his high school diploma. There was nothing to be done about it. His class had finally graduated a month ago by government decree. The honorable diploma was now hanging on the living room wall with the Minister of Education's signature on it and all. Chingolo was right. Never having gone to school was unquestionably the best part of his schooling. He could be thankful to the army for that, at least. He learned to play soccer in the streets. He knew how to read. Now he was writing. What more could he have gotten out of school? Just walking the city streets was enough. One learned more. One learned better.

Then don't eat. Starve to death. See if I care.

A walk with Chingolo on sunny afternoons. Always with the parrot on his left shoulder. The parrot would flap its wings every once in a while and insult passersby, especially fat ladies dressed in black, the perverse bird. *All against the wall!* Chingolo was worried that he might be arrested for writing. They'll put you on one of the lists. But I have to. And Chingolo yelled at him that he was a lost cause and muttered something about postglacial readaptation in Mesoamerica. Stop the bullshit, Chingolo. It's not bullshit. Evidence has been found in the coproliths of parasite-infested Huaca priests.

On the afternoon of the lengthy conversation about the positive and negative aspects of the flea, Máximo went over to The Last Goodbye to have a beer. He was taken aback to find a huge color TV in the middle of the cantina. It was the first he had seen in the last five years. Since Karen's Sony. He watched, everybody was watching it. Three toothless men. One without a left arm. Three missing feet, one left and two right. Fingers and right arms missing. A pair of ears. A nose. Some eyes, but not many. Everybody complaining about the TV. We don't want to watch television. What people go to cantinas for is to guzzle. And that program is terrible. I wonder what they will think about it afterwards. Máximo knew that there was no color television in the country. Then the light dawned. It was in

English. And at that very moment the channel identification came on. It was from San Antonio. Máximo asked the bartender what it was all about. Technicians arrived and installed it. They said it was a gift. They set it on this channel because it was good for the customers, they said. It would re-educate them. Máximo looking at them. They kept on complaining. We don't even understand that language. Who gives a damn about those blonde, screechy women. If they'd just turn it off. Máximo asked them why somebody didn't get up and do it. They all looked at one another. Eyelashes flapped. Mouths opened and shut without a sound emerging. They kept on watching, turning around, shrugging, some chins sunken on chests. Somebody called for another drink. Somebody else tried to crack a joke.

Máximo walked over to the TV. *I do love you,* the blond man was saying. *Then why do you do this to me?* the blond woman replied. There were a lot of buttons. Volume. Horizontal. Vertical. On, off. Máximo pushed it. The TV whined like a spent electric bulb and went dark gray. Everybody looked at the dead TV. He started toward the door. Everybody applauded and whistled, toasted the dead TV and him. Somebody shouted at him that he hoped they didn't give him a scholarship to Panama. The parrot answered *All against the wall!*

Máximo strolled down the street. He looked at the dried-up leaves blown by the wind. He imagined, yes, all the beggars dragging themselves along the Street of Sighs with broken legs, hunting the elusive crust of bread. He stepped on some glass and noted all the uncollected garbage. The leading social theoretician was passing by across the street in his wheelchair. Máximo tried to imagine what it would feel like to be a leading social theoretician. To be in a wheelchair. Life. Closing in on him sometimes, he felt, from every direction. One does what one can. Máximo kicked an empty can trying to score in the opening of the sewer. Missed by an inch. The can banged against the curb and bounded the width of the street. The leading social theoretician was rolling along by some dead bushes and a withered tree. Máximo saw it, the soldiers jumped out from behind the dead bushes and the withered tree. He could see the machine guns perfectly, glinting in the afternoon sunlight. Saw how they emptied them, one by one, into the leading social theoretician's body. A priest heard the shots and ran to ring the church bells. Máximo looked, Máximo was unable to move. The leading theoretician's body hung over the side of the blood-covered wheelchair. Máximo ran to ask the soldiers why. Because the comandante of the guerrillas had been killed in an accident on the highway the other night, they told him. Turcios, the Turcios, oh Turcios, *adiós, adiós, adiós,* Turcios. They had to use up the unused bullets on somebody. The parrot screeched *All against the wall!* The soldiers laughed nervously and disappeared behind the dead bushes and the withered tree. They didn't care if he told what he had seen. They couldn't care less. Because he was unable to tell. Words were illegal. The bells kept ringing, ringing. The body hung over the side of the wheelchair. Máximo was glad to see that they hadn't broken the man's glasses. He bit into his pacifier and moved on.

To be or not to be. That is the bullet.

He turned the corner. It was colder, the sky was cloudy. Now almost hiding the sun. A huge rat ran in front of him, a hand hanging from its mouth. A baby's hand, was it? Máximo wasn't sure. He was no longer sure of anything. Things kept happening, kept happening. Thorn plants grew out of the cracks in the pavement. He recalled how the Indians' Holy Week ends without Resurrection. He remembered María Tecún. Maybe pay María Tecún a visit. Start from there? Start somewhere. But he hadn't even done that. He had to start somewhere. The bells kept ringing, ringing. Another block, another turn. By Las Conchas park. He kept walking. He heard the screams. Were those screams he was hearing? Soldiers were already in the park, the beauty queen thrown to the ground. It was the beauty queen, wasn't it? They had torn off her blouse. Large, full breasts. Aggressive ones? A soldier was kneeling next to her. He was tearing off her nipples with his teeth. Was he tearing off her nipples with his teeth? She was screaming and screaming and screaming and screaming and screaming. The soldier had blood all over his face. Máximo stopped. There were other soldiers around, too. And they smiled at him. He stopped. They smiled at him. The other one kept biting her. Large, full breasts. Aggressive ones? She was screaming, twisting, screaming, twisting. She was collaborating with the guerrillas the soldiers told him and shrugged. The parrot screeched at them *All against the wall!* They laughed nervously and turned to look at the comrade who was biting her. The bells kept ringing, ringing.

Time passed and as was to be expected the number of deaths climbed. Máximo had closed

176

himself in his room. He saw nobody. Ate little. Talked only to his parrot.

Eagle Beak, my dearest, have you seen Máximo lately?

Eagle Beak I'll be, a parrot no. And you? Are you expecting him?

Expecting a child? No. Am I putting on weight? Tell the truth.

Actually, I meant...

Have a *champurrada*.

You're terrible.

Because I have a loose tongue, they say.

And more. You're a temptress, you daughter of capitalism.

Irresistible, aren't we? And afterwards they say that one...

But I'm leaving. Carry on awaiting your Prince Máximo...

Me, wait? Not for him or anyone, love.

In that case...

Dunk your *champurrada* in the coffee.

I don't like crumbs.

You make me nervous.

Is that all?

Well, among other things.

What things?

Succulent things.

Want them? Do you really want them?

Just intellectual curiosity. Desire to know.

To desire is to do.

Just a mental act to me. Go find the boy of action.

Forget my valiant prince and don't you chicken out on me.

Such strong talk, woman!

We gringas are salacious.

Salacious, contumacious, predacious, and voracious....

But efficacious where it matters and with us no need to wait for the priest's blessing.

The thing is that we are underdeveloped.

I've know some very well-developed parts.

Of course, one developed part attracts another.

Enough, don't push it, you really like to probe...

Only in the interest of science.

Like a good bourgeois. Always in love affairs with hot little ideas but when push comes to shove, no dice.

Insults. Nothing but insults.

What do you mean insults? It's true. They're right in killing your kind first.

All that education for nothing.

Hooray for nothing.

And to end up alone roaming the streets, doing the rounds of bars and sadness? In every direction, without direction, without sense, without pride...

Without anything.

My tropical temperament prevents me. *Adiós*.

Where are you sailing off to, dreamboat.

When the CIA man was killed, the government announced a grand official funeral to placate Washington which was demanding redress. The whores' strike had ended. Every potential victim had been victimized. And it was so difficult to dislodge the guerrillas from the mountains. When the whores' strike ended the soldiers had better things to do. "Spider" Arana had a serious dilemma on his hands. His cabinet met in emergency session. They decided to try to gain time by holding the biggest, most lavish funeral ever seen, until they were able to think of whom to blame. How could we be so stupid? the Minister of the Interior said. We should have saved the leading social theoretician for it. The funeral services were to be held in the great banquet hall of the Ministry of Culture, no less. The entire diplomatic corps would be invited. Various foreign dignitaries. Women with large breasts. The CIA man had been quite a connoisseur in that area. Selected entertainers and intellectuals whose faith in the democratic process was well-known had been invited to entertain the guests.

Máximo wanted to attend. He ran to Amarena's house with his yellow pages. Chingolo was still there explaining the differences between the observations of Auddablika and Bhabravya, to say nothing of Vatsyayana. I wanna go, I wanna go, yelled Máximo. And Amarena threw a pillow at his head.

Interrupting my Kamasutra instruction like that! Who do you think you are?

But Máximo went on yelling I wanna go, I wanna go and Chingolo was forced to admit that Amarena had nothing more to learn about eating mangos.

Go where? To the funeral? To the funeral? Go? Do you want to kill me? Kill us all? Do you think they'll like it? That they will accept you there? That they'll just stand around? Sucking their thumbs? That they'll do nothing? Nothing? Nothing?

I'd like to take some of these along, he said, waving his yellow sheets. Amarena smiled. Chingolo shrugged. It's forbidden to write but not to read, said Máximo. I don't know what time it is, but I know it's time. And what about being prudent? asked Chingolo. *All against the wall!* screeched the parrot. Amarena's limousine was parked outside the U.S. Embassy that night. She came out of there around daybreak with a handful of passes to the funeral.

Máximo, it's suicide.

What choice is there? One must pass from words to action, mustn't one? Let them make their inferences. And if they don't, what of it?

Máximo told Pacha. Pacha told Rodri. Rodri wanted to tell somebody, but who? They were all very excited and approved. They were worried, though. We're going to end up in shit creek, they said. Amarena gave them their passes. Plus extras for their soccer pals. The banquet hall wasn't exactly a stadium but she had enough. And she could ask for more from the old man if she wanted, she said with great pride. And if not she could always pay a call on the man in gray who worked at the Blue Cross building. And she was getting all her friends the whores together. They would all be there, too, she promised. It was going to be a very special group of mourners. Select. It will be worth it even if we do end up in the creek, said Máximo.

It was going to be a funeral such as the city had not seen since General Castle Cannons came out on his balcony. The Avenue of the Alliance for Progress, where the unfortunate man had lived, was completely adorned with black drapes and white flowers. The idea had even come up of renaming the street for him. His body was lying in state upon an enormous urn in the main hall of the National

Palace. It was being attended by little boys in green berets who changed guard every half hour.

The next day they moved the casket up to the banquet hall. The exclusive invitations indicated that the cortege would depart for the cemetery immediately upon conclusion of the grand ceremony.

With the temporary stands set up on three sides, the banquet hall looked more like a gymnasium. A white wall completed the rectangle. The casket exactly in the center of the floor covered entirely by rare white orchids. At the ends, two huge candelabras with fat candles more than six feet high. And similarly the card of condolence with a narrow black border and General "Spider" Arana's signature lying on the casket. Men in white tuxedoes moved among the crowd passing out glasses of champagne.

The guests of honor, the cabinet, army officers, and the diplomatic corps seated on the right. Selected entertainers and intellectuals on the left. In the center, all the other people lucky enough to have obtained passes. Máximo recognized his friends, all already present, many friends. It would work out.

Long speeches were delivered. The Archbishop, holding hands with the sexton, offered a prayer. A general with a long face enumerated the highlights of the splendid work accomplished by the deceased. A blond man with a thick accent stood up to announce that the Smithsonian Institute had just purchased the bullet-riddled car.

Two and a half hours after the opening, the master of ceremonies announced the first entertainer. A skinny painter, but so skinny he looked like a skeleton. Máximo knew him, of course.

He was the youngest of the Minister of Health's 23 children. He proceeded to the center of the hall. There was a hush. Suddenly, he stopped dead in his tracks, made a half-turn, and tore off his clothes. Black tights underneath. And he broke into a leaping dance around the casket, springing into the air, he fell and rolled on the ground in an acrobatic arched turn that brought him back to his feet. He looked as if he was having a series of epileptic fits. He disappeared behind a small door to reappear seconds later with an enormous bouquet of balloons, which he dragged along the floor, they did not float. Of all colors, red, yellow, blue, green, violet. He lined them up on the floor parallel to the casket and recommenced his *danse macabre*. He picked up the red balloon and threw it against the wall. It burst upon contact staining the wall with red paint that began to run down the surface. He threw himself to the ground in Japanese fashion bowing to the audience which responded with reflex applause and he started dancing again. This time he selected a yellow balloon. And he repeated the previous action, identically, smearing the wall with yellow paint. He continued in the same way, receiving applause each time he kissed the ground. Finally, only one balloon was left, a red one. He contemplated it, launched into his dance, then stopped beside the balloon. He picked it up, changed his mind, put it back on the floor. No. He picked it up again, it was terribly heavy, he mimed, lifting it high above him with a tremendous effort. Suddenly, he let go and it dropped on his head bursting open. Red paint streamed over his entire body. The public broke into loud applause and shouts of appreciation. Dripping, he bowed happily, throwing kisses to his admirers. He ran to the wall to sign the design with huge black letters, after which he disappeared through the same little door. Protracted applause.

The master of ceremonies was just about to announce the next performer when Máximo jumped up and ran to the center of the hall.

I'm going on. It's my turn.

His action took everyone by surprise. What's happening? A number of low voices murmured. What's going on? But no one moved. The master of ceremonies, what to do? This was a funeral after all. He had strict orders. Be sure everything goes smoothly. The generals wanted no embarrassment before so many foreign dignitaries. What to do? The master of ceremonies, with great composure, smiled and made his announcement, this artist would present an improvisation. That is what he said and quickly retired. Scattered applause.

Máximo paced from one point to another, hands behind his back, chin on his breast. As though deep in meditation, thinking. Complete silence in the hall. Máximo looked up at the ceiling, not at the audience, and began to speak very slowly, deliberately.

Not long ago, Yon Sosa said that in the mountains. machine guns, rifles, and grenades were not the principal weapons

He paused, cleared his throat. He had mentioned a forbidden name. There was murmuring in the stands, the generals, purple in the face, swallowing saliva.

They merely provide a safe basis for contact with the peasants. The principal weapon is words.

The murmuring rose in volume. Máximo stopped talking. Suddenly, he turned, ran toward the casket and jumped up on it, mashing the flowers and pulling out a handful of yellow pages from under his shirt. There were shouts and people jumped up from their seats. The soccer players and the whores stood up to applaud while Máximo shook the handful of papers over his head. Women fainted and men covered their faces with their hands. Whistling and insults from everywhere in the hall.

I am going to read you a story with true words. Its title is "The CIA Man" and in all humbleness I dedicate it to the man upon whose casket I now stand.

Suddenly his voice was flowing, making itself felt above the hysterical outcries of the audience, a controlled voice, lyrical, melodious, that dominated all other voices.

"Fish are no longer to be seen in the Motagua River. The fishermen have caught too many bodies by now in their nets. The beautiful teacher without a head, the castrated man, the peasant from Salamá with pins in his eyes. The ordinary citizen is confused by all these things. Some ordinary citizens accept the existence of death but deny the reality of the corpses. A conspiracy of fear, they say. Others accept the existence of the corpses but deny the reality of a conspiracy. After all, accidents happen. The confusion grows. The CIA man is asked his opinion. He takes a long drag on his Camel. For some, beauty is an escape, he says. The ordinary citizen is confused. Some accept the existence of the CIA man as an abstraction but deny the reality of his being. But it is well known that others do not agree."

The audience had quieted down. They had never heard anything like this. Was it a joke? An insult? What did it mean? It sounded like a speech in honor of the dead man but they weren't sure.

"The CIA man is driving a red Alfa Romeo alongside the Motagua. Fishing should be illegal in rivers, he thinks. That's what oceans were for. They do everything upside down in these countries. He imagines dropping a few bodies in the river to scare the fishermen. He could see it so clearly in his mind's eye. The calm waters bearing a beautiful teacher without a head, a castrated man, a peasant from Salamá with pins in his eyes. It's possible, he thought. And then he saw the men and the woman."

Everybody began to feel uncomfortable but nobody knew what to do. The army officers refused to stop the performance unless an offense was committed against the diplomatic corps. After all, its being on the program meant it was a number that had received prior approval, and the master of ceremonies had introduced it as part of the program. The diplomatic corps, unfamiliar with the strange funerary customs of underdeveloped countries, refused to react. Some were enjoying the spectacle, in any case, true admirers that they were of anything fresh in the entertainment line. And the master of ceremonies refused to stop the number without a direct order from the generals, fearing for his life if he admitted an error. Máximo went on reading.

"The ordinary citizens consider other possibilities. Perhaps there are no bodies and no conspiracy. The papers had exaggerated before, on occasions. No, say others. A conspiracy must exist even if there are no bodies. Otherwise, it would make no sense. Most of the ordinary citizens are in agreement that the conspiracy theory would gain credence if the existence of corpses could be established. But others are opposed claiming that maybe there are bodies but not many or that the forms of mutilation aren't original enough. Some argue that this is an unorthodox position, against protocol. And there were also those who are not in agreement with the method of investigation used. Lastly, one ordinary citizen admits that he neither believes nor disbelieves anything, that he doesn't even understand what is going on. All the other ordinary citizens agreed with that."

Máximo stopped reading for a moment. Amarena began to applaud. The generals looked at one another? There was no sex in the story. Why waste time listening to a story that didn't have juicy sex in it?

"The CIA man mused. Here I am, assigned to instructing the police in sophisticated weaponry and stuff like that. But it's really a nice, clear morning, he mused, I'm driving this gorgeous Alfa Romeo along the banks of the Motagua River and I don't even have to smoke Camels to confuse the ordinary citizen. But still, this isn't Virginia. He took a deep breath of the clean, fresh air. Nonetheless, being the CIA man isn't all bad. As long as one suffers through occasional moments of contrition. He tried to bring on a moment of contrition. Will I ever get out of this country? And if I do, will I ever get out of this job? And if I do get out? No, I'll never make it. He had been trained to perform acts of self-examination of exquisite quality. Will I be able to get used to the fact that my forehead drips sweat all the time? Will my son forgive me some day? Will he understand? Does it matter? What matters? He felt quite relaxed immediately after his moment of contrition. And then he saw the men and the woman."

Should they stop him? They would stop him at the first sign that the gringo ambassador was angry. But the old man wasn't reacting. How the fuck could they know whether they should stop the number or not, if the old sonofabitch didn't react?

"There had been some kind of confrontation. But the ordinary citizens weren't impressed. An ordinary citizen spoke to another ordinary citizen. Boring, boring, boring, I'm telling you. No blood, not even one dead. And they surrendered immediately. I was going along Servility Street when I heard the first shots. I ran but when I got to the avenue it was all over. They had just surrendered. They had their hands up. The CIA man had directed the whole operation with a Camel between his lips. His eyes were on the stolen Alfa Romeo they had caught them in. A fat old woman dug an elbow into my chest. They took them away in a paddy wagon. The CIA man left driving the Alfa Romeo. There was no blood. The crowd jeered when the police refused to crack their heads open. Boring, boring, boring. By now the CIA man must be cruising along the bank of the Motagua River."

One of the generals bent over to whisper in his lover's ear that he had never liked literature because it was always so difficult to understand what the hell it meant. She agreed.

"The CIA man left the motor running and got out of the car gun in hand. What are you doing with that woman? Her lower lip was swollen. The CIA man noted that they carried only machetes, smiled, took out a Camel. She was wearing a khaki shirt and he wasn't sure whether she had a brassiere on underneath He hoped she didn't. He could see the soft breasts in his mind's eye. We're honorable men, sir, and they proceeded to identify themselves. Their ID definitely identified them as honorable men. A government seal made it official. She had a bruise on her forehead and her slacks were muddy and torn. The CIA man wondered whether they had raped her. Did you rape this woman? he asked. No, they answered. We are honorable men. What are you doing with her then? We're going to cut her head off and throw her in the river because she's one of them. But the CIA man knew she was not. Nobody with such aggressive breasts could be one of them. The honorable men asked themselves what aggressive breasts were but the CIA man wouldn't let them see. Don't look, he told them or I'll shoot you. The honorable men agreed not to look."

The Archbishop turned white and buried his face in the sexton's chest. Aha! the generals said, it is obscene after all. Now we know what to ban when he finishes and we will ban it. Because they didn't want to interrupt. All of them wanted to hear more about those aggressive breasts.

Commotion. There will be a commotion if the question is not satisfactorily answered, the ordinary citizens said. It wasn't actually the corpses that bothered them but rather the absence of heads, genitals, eyes. It is hard to accept fragmentation in a society struggling to integrate itself. All the ordinary men were agreed although some asked themselves what kind of commotion. Just commotion, the others said. Ordinary commotion.

The U.S. Ambassador didn't move. He was so well-mannered. Maybe he even *knew* what the story meant. He was *so* well-mannered. All the generals were dying to hear more about the breasts. So exciting! So obscene!

"The CIA man motioned her into the car with his gun. But she's one of them, the honorable men said. I'm the CIA man, he said, and I know that she isn't. I always know if somebody is one of them or not. Okay, then, the honorable men replied, but don't say we didn't warn you. The CIA man drove the car away in a cloud of dust. You're probably a country school teacher. Yes, she said. You're beautiful. Yes, she said. You aren't one of them. No, she said. I can see you in my mind without your shirt on. You have aggressive breasts, very firm. Yes, she said. Would you like a Camel?"

The silence was complete, now. All that could be heard was heavy breathing in the stands on the right. The Archbishop peeped through the spaces between his fingers.

"The ordinary citizens are confused. Three more bodies have appeared in the river. A beautiful teacher without a head, a castrated man, a peasant from Salamá with pins in his eyes. The confusion is increasing. The CIA man is asked for his opinion. He takes a long drag on his Camel. You know, he says, for some, beauty is an escape."

He stopped reading. He remained there standing on the casket. Waiting, waiting for the reaction. Silence. Nobody moved. Not a sound anywhere. He tucked the yellow sheets back inside his shirt.

Finally, all at once, the center stands burst into prolonged, resounding, applause. The whores stood up on their seats, throwing kisses, stamping their feet on the chairs, yelling, applauding, applauding. The soccer players, too, hurrahs could be heard, Viva Máximo! Everybody standing and whistling, hats in the air. The U.S. Ambassador was getting up too, he stood up. He looked at the generals. They, professionally analyzing just how aggressive those breasts might have been. Like the beauty queen's, perhaps? The Ambassador's face was changing color, going from paper white to cobalt blue. He tried to speak but could produce no words. His throat expanded and contracted, his eyes threatening to pop out of their sockets, but not a word came out. Finally, he brandished a fist in their direction and ran out leaving his hat behind. A lieutenant ran after him, the hat in his hand.

Máximo laughed. Pandemonium in the center stands, wonderful pandemonium! Groups of people arguing about what they had just heard. The first fight broke out. Somebody threw a glass of champagne in somebody else's wife's face, a sound of broken glass, two bodies rolling on the floor, crashing against the metal chairs.

All the doors slammed open at once. Soldiers with machine guns came running into the hall. Amarena saw them. She grabbed the hand of the whore closest to her and they both ran towards the center of the room. She began kissing the first soldier she found. All the other whores followed her example, jumping down from the central stands, catching hold of a soldier, embracing him. The Archbishop was hustled out of the place by the sexton. Some of the women were starting to strip. Exposed breasts could already be seen. Men were jumping down from all the stands, too, fighting with the soldiers over possession of the bare-breasted women, trying to get their share of the booty. All the officers were yelling Attention! but nobody paid any. The soccer players kicked the heads of the soldiers. They couldn't compete with Culiche or Pinulita but they played well enough to score and left their opponents stretched out all around. The men were rolling all over the floor. And the women. The soldiers were losing their pants. Their underwear sliding down. One couple rolling on the floor, he on top, she on top, he on top, knocked over the honored agent's casket. It fell off to the right, bursting open to reveal the petrified smile that creased the waxen countenance. A dazed whore began to kiss the corpse. Several soldiers managed to get off a few shots into the air but nobody wanted to hear them. Somebody shoved a chilly machine-gun barrel up a naked soldier's ass. One of the giant candles fell to the floor and rolled onto a pile of discarded clothes. Some of which soon began to smoke. Terrified shouts went up from all around. Fire! Fire! Flames began to dance, licking at the wooden stands, the floor, tentatively at first, and then with greater abandon, clothing, people doubling over with coughing fits, galloping towards the nearest exits, stepping on one another, pushing, kicking, biting, running naked, running scratched and bitten and bruised through, over, between everything, the flames leaping high into the air, supple, catlike pirouettes blackening the ceiling, devouring the wooden floor, the casket, the smiling dead body.

Chaos developing outside. The news already out, tongues wagging throughout the city. Smoke already visible in the distance. Fire trucks everywhere, howling, everywhere. Half-naked people on the sidewalk, fits of coughing, of asthma, of nerves. Sporadic bursts of machine-gun fire could be heard as in a dream. Excited men chasing naked whores through the streets. Sweating officers driving away enraged in their jeeps.

The fire was under control two and a half hours later and there was a price on Máximo's head. He had not been seen, had disappeared, from that eternal moment when the whores jumped into the middle of the hall.

Dusk fell. The sirens audible in the remotest corners of the city. Ambulances dashing madly in all directions. Jeeps full of soldiers in all the streets. Nothing on the radio but the inevitable martial music. News flashes. People left work early. The city began to appear deserted.

A knock on the door early in the evening. Máximo's mother about to throw some beans into a pan.

Who's there?

We have some questions to ask you.

Oh, yeh? Who is it?

Police.

Why didn't you say so in the first place? Cat got your tongue?

She opened the door. A dozen men stormed into the entrance pushing her up against the wall. She recognized the machine guns.

Where's your son? Answer!

192

She was thinking that they ought to wash behind the ears. And clean their teeth. Especially their teeth.

The men fanned out through the house. She watched them running into the bedrooms, the living room. Her son? Had he done something? Her darling, her treasure? One of the men kept his his hand on her shoulder and fired question after question at her.

Jesus, Mary, and Joseph! Shut up, young man, and listen to me. I'm kind of old now for these games! You tell me! What are these, these, men doing? Barging into my house like this! What do you want with my son? You tell me.

The man slapped her in the face. She stared at him she couldn't believe it, her eyes bigger than ever, her mouth open, a little cut on her lower lip.

What nerve, you animal.

Shut your mouth and answer, old woman.

She slapped him full in the face. He stared at her he couldn't believe it, his eyes bigger than ever, his mouth open. She slapped him again.

Learn to respect your elders, young man!

He lowered his eyes. She crossed her arms talking to herself. And then she saw what the others were doing.

They had slashed the couch with their knives. All the stuffing had burst out. The doors of the cabinets were wrenched off. She ran after them, yelling, insulting them. The man guarding her didn't move.

She went into the kitchen. Glasses, plates, pots. Everything on the floor. A man cutting open the bottom of a sack. The beans spilling out, an explosion of beans. She threw herself on him, furious, clawing at his back, jumping to bite him on the neck. He turned and punched her in the stomach with his fist. She doubled over and fell. In immediate succession, rice, salt, coffee, all on the floor in a heap. And then the cans, all the cans tumbling down.

When she finally managed to drag herself out of the kitchen, all the furniture was piled up in the patio. She could see, perfectly clearly, the chairs lying there with their insides torn out. Surrounded with flowers, the sad daisies and carnations and begonias. And the springs. Jumping every which way near the dusty ferns. All the mattresses were there. The straw could be seen protruding where the knives had perforated. The living room carpet. The dining-room table with the legs broken off. All the chests and the clothes. Curtains. Máximo's desk. His grandfather's old desk. Golden mahogany. Protection from the bombs. Sole witness of generations. And the yellow pages, her son, oh, how yellow those sheets of paper were.

She tried to get up. Her back was aching. Her head. Her legs trembling. A man opened a can and emptied the contents on the mound of memories. She yelled at them. Yelled, yelling. Her stomach hurt terribly every time but she kept on yelling. The man tossed the empty can aside. It bounded into a corner behind the begonias. She managed to get to her feet pulling herself up on the kitchen door, inch by inch. The man took a box of matches from his shirt pocket. The desk was in the middle. In the back the empty bird cages, for so long now, memories of memories, empty so many years now. Everything coming to an end. Everything advancing toward nothingness. She took a few shaky steps through the corridor hanging onto the column. The man dropped the match to the mute surprise of the cockroaches and the sobs of the spiders.

Goddamn sons of bitches!

They waited until the fire had died. Leaving the embers still glowing. Silently they divided up the little money and few jewels they had found.

She clutched the column. Without a word. Her eyes on the ashes of the old desk. It made no sense. They came over to her. She did not look up. They removed her arms from around the column. She did not resist. They led her to the door. She went with them. They closed the front door with its gilt knocker, the lion's head. She never noticed. The youngest of them ran politely ahead to open the rear door of the unmarked car. She didn't resist. They helped her into the car.

The sirens howled all night long. Army trucks and jeeps invaded all sectors of the city. The few cars that ventured out were stopped and searched. They were looking for the soccer players and the whores. Helicopters lent by the Canal Zone were circling and circling the city directing operations over loudspeakers that kept everybody from sleeping, from having nightmares. Some streets were shot up. The startled passersby ducking between the bullets, clawing at doors and windows, pleading to be let in. Paddy wagons sealed off street after street. Hundreds of arrests were made. Where was Máximo hiding?

It was he on the front page of the next day's papers. Electrifying headlines. Sensational articles. Statements from witnesses. Photos. Hostile editorials. Paid ads denouncing him. Condemnations by the Church. Máximo had become a menace to society. Treason, said the headlines. The government's anger knew no bounds. Pressure from Washington mounted. Something had to be done. Fast. Fill up the jails. Arrest everybody whose name begins with M. Martínez. Mateos. Miranda. Morales. They promised, if they caught Máximo, to tear out his tongue and cut off his left hand.

The Marines had now landed. To protect American homes and property. To guarantee the peace and security of the diplomatic community. There were Marines in the Embassy and the consulate. The young tow-heads could be seen at the Monsanto and Texaco headquarters. There were Marines at the electric company and the fruit company. There were freckle-faces and redheads on the railroads. There were Marines at the Blue Cross building where a new group of technical advisors had just arrived bearing gifts. There were Marines at Kentucky Fried Chicken and the Union Church.

A limousine stopped in front of the Union Church. The chauffeur jumped out to open the rear door. A pistol butt sticking out of his waistband. A woman in black covered with an enormous veil stepped out of the car. The courteous chauffeur took her by the arm and helped her to the church door, saluting the alert Marines. They snapped to attention.

The Reverend's daughter.

She smiled at them. She entered. The church empty, not a soul. Only one man. But he was the janitor. He kept on sweeping, no problem there. Amarena slipped him a one-quetzal bill as she went by. He took it without raising his eyes. She opened a

side door. A short corridor led to a patio closed in by
thick stone walls. A massive fountain in the center
with stone benches around it. She threw some coins
into the fountain and continued on to the door at
the other end.

Amarena?

She entered, closed the door behind her, ran to
embrace him. She did not look well to him. It's
nothing, just nerves, she said. Let's face it, the
situation is pretty hairy, isn't it? Yes, but it's one
thing to. And something else to. No, man. Aside
from the fact that they want to tear out your tongue
and cut off your left hand, everything's fine. Cool, as
your intrepid guards sunning themselves outside
would say. Stop trying to be cute with me, dammit.
Shit, don't I have the right to if I feel like it? You
think you're a brown-skinned Superman of the
Third World, all puffed up because the whole police
force is after your ass, but I'm the one out there
putting my neck on the line for you. She told him
his house had been searched. My mother! She
assured him that his mother was alright, that she
had been sent word, anything that came into her
head. I knew it. Don't lie to me about this, hear.
She's hiding, too, Amarena said, and can't see you
before you leave. Of course, how could she see me?
They burned your papers. The desk. Everything. He
changed his tone. What to think? How far to believe
her? But, what the hell. What's the difference. It was
no joke. Things were very tough. But what could
you do, just live through it. See what happens. Learn
to laugh it off with your guts in a knot and your
mouth all dry. So what's the problem? Aren't you

proud of the scholarship to Panama they're offering you?

Are you sure they can't do anything to you?

Man, me a gringa and with diplomatic status and all?

What about the others? Chingolo?

Alive and bushy-tailed. They're only after people whose names begin with M.

She explained to him the arrangements she was making to get him out of the country. He not mentioning his doubts, silent. She kept talking, explaining details that he didn't understand. He was in her hands.

Amarena, did you notice my face?

How could I not? You look a fright.

No, stupid. My skin. Take a look at my skin.

It's almost clear. It was the first thing I noticed when I came in.

Amarena, what am I going to do?

You'll split and chase after your elusive words and leave me with this mess.

Do you think I'll be back?

So now I'm your gypsy fortune teller. How the hell do I know?

What about you?

She didn't answer. He gazed long at her face, taking in its every detail. A faint smile rose to her lips. He embraced her again. She saw the tears in his eyes and burst out laughing.

Don't go getting all mushy on me, now. Careful you don't mess up the finale.

Dammit, I'm about to step out of this shit forever, maybe. Don't I have a right?

Sentimentality is nearly as boring as talking about the weather. Remember? Is perversity what it's all about?

Laughing once more, hugging, kissing. Tickling each other. Hands fondling each other.

You're pissing in your pants but you think you're hot shit because of what you did, right?

Look. I had to do something, fuck!

The enormous fuck.

The gigantic fuck.

The global fuck.

The universal fuck.

The supreme fuck.

Amarena, listen. There's something else I have to do before I go.

What?

Pay María Tecún a visit.

Sonofa. Man, you sure can be a pain. How right they are: You give a Latin an inch, he takes a mile.

Stick it in, take it out. Life here is "Stick it to them or get stuck." Don't tell me you haven't taken notice of our booming stick industry?

The sirens didn't stop screeching all day long. Army trucks and jeeps kept all sectors of the city under siege. The few vehicles circulating were overturned and set on fire. Every house in the city searched. Another fleet of helicopters was expected from Panama. The sounds of gunfire increased. Thousands of arrests made. Where was Máximo hiding?

Late afternoon, a knocking at the door. Chingolo was putting on his windbreaker at the time. He was to have a strategy meeting with Pacha and Rodri at The Last Goodbye. He heard the knocking again.

Before he could get to the door a burst of a machine gun fire blew out the lock. A dozen men in filthy clothes entered. Chingolo stood in the middle of the corridor thinking that if he were an entrepreneur he would seriously consider going into the laundry business. They all pointed gun barrels at his chest.

Let's go.

I'm afraid there's some mistake, gentlemen. My name doesn't begin with M.

There's no mistake, sonofabitch. We know you conspired with that other individual to smear our government in the eyes of the world the other day at the Ministry of Culture. So don't play innocent. We know you're a ringleader. You're done for.

I? Ringleader? But, gentlemen...

A gun butt in the stomach silenced him. The neighbors saw him being led to the back seat of an unmarked car and watched it disappear out of sight.

Pacha and Rodri were at The Last Goodbye. Martial law had been declared. Only institutions for moral purposes were permitted to remain open: churches, bars, and government-regulated whorehouses. The customers of The Last Goodbye were watching television. Three toothless. One without a left arm. Three feet missing. One left and two right. Fingers and right arms missing. A pair of ears. A nose. A few eyes but not many. Everybody was complaining about the TV.

Jeezus! The time has come. What a crazy fucking world.

Has the time come? Sure, I can see. Yes.

But I'd like to know where, primerically. And give me an answer secondarically.

Me, too, yes, I'd like to know, too. But we have no time to lose.

Seated in their regular corner unable to see anything anymore because of the smoke. The jukebox, never ending its whining, whined on.

> And you left me memories
> That I can never in my life forget
> When I was surer of you than ever
> Your treachery wounded me to the soul.
> I swear by God
> you'll have your punishment
> For what you did to me.

They drove all night. Chingolo was afraid. Were they taking him to the infamous La Palma concentration camp? Near Río Hondo. He knew, yes, the smells, it was some time since they had left the city. Still dark when they finally stopped.

They took him to *Intelligence*. A fat man with a bushy mustache, his shirt open to the navel, was reading a comic book. As soon as he saw him, he began, the questions. He gave his name. He admitted that he knew Máximo. He did, didn't he? He confessed that he did not agree that the story should end with the line: For some, beauty is an escape. It seemed to him a loose sentence and a bit out of key with the rest of the story. Besides its being vague. He said that personally he would have liked to see a multiplicity of CIA men in the story to reinforce more strongly their robotesque nature, completely removed from reality. But he understood that Máximo had been under great pressure to finish it in time and the little tale wasn't so bad as it stood. The officer roared something unintelligible, spit on the floor, and went back to reading his comic book. The men who had brought him in took him away.

A limousine stopped in front of the Blue Cross building. The chaffeur jumped out to open the rear door. A pistol butt was sticking out of his belt. A woman dressed in black covered with an enormous veil stepped out of the car. The courteous chaffeur took her by the arm and helped her to the door of the building, saluting the alert Marines. They snapped to attention.

The Reverend's daughter.

She smiled at them. She entered. A tall, square man in a gray suit was waiting in the corridor. He had curly blond hair and sucked impatiently on a pipe.

My dear Mr. Wright! Lovely to see you again.

They took him to a cell. Forced him to turn around, his face against the wall. He got ready for them to begin beating him. Instead, they searched his pockets. They took all his money. They left him alone.

Máximo tried to lie down against the wall but the parrot wouldn't stop nipping at his nose and ears.

They returned later and told him to stand with his face against the wall. He told them he had no more money. They covered his head with a hood that had holes for the eyes and mouth. It was damp and dirty. Fortunately his nose stuck out quite far. He complained that besides the lack of facilities they were keeping him awake. He explained that his metabolism required eight hours of uninterrupted sleep daily. They took him out of the cell and made him run and run, pulling him by the arms. They forced him to run through long halls, run up stairs, run around a room, run down other stairs, run around the courtyard, run through some strange archways, run around a column a number of times. His nose was cold, very cold.

The parrot kept scratching and biting. He gave it a smack. *All against the wall,* screeched the parrot.

They stopped. More men around him. He could hear their footsteps, their voices, feel their presence. They stripped him. He protested. He apologized for limiting himself to heterosexual relations, it was primarily because he was shy, but noted that he intellectually accepted bisexuality as the ideal and a model. It seemed as though day was about to break. They tied damp cloths to his wrists and ankles. He felt good after the exercise. He wasn't in such bad physical shape after all. They pushed him onto a mattress that lay on a metal frame. The cold felt pleasant but the metal was uncomfortable. They spread his legs, he blushed, and they tied his wrists and ankles. He thought of the forgotten afternoon he introduced Amarena to Máximo. They dumped a pail of water over him and then threw wet rags over his whole body. Now the cold began to penetrate to his bones! Would the sun come out, perhaps? His jaw trembled. His body was all gooseflesh. They began to play a record. At full volume. He didn't care for the piece and asked if they didn't have some Mozart. But he would settle for Beethoven. And then they began the electric shocks. To say nothing of Vivaldi.

The limousine returned home. The butler ran out to give her the message that Pacha and Rodri had left. They had gone into hiding. They heard about Chingolo in the cantina. The butler told them where to go and hide.

They asked a question and then the electric shock. Each time the current came on, the men jumped around the mattress applauding and shouting twist! twist! twist! The recording was in English and they didn't understand the words.

She got in touch with all her contacts. Help him? Get him out? Save him? They promised to do everything possible.

Everything bursting out. Jerking his kidneys, wrenching his guts. Everything. Bursting out. In the distance, screams. Applause. If they would only turn over the record. They applauded. If they would only turn over the record.

The limousine stopped in front of the Union Church. The chauffeur jumped. A woman dressed in black came out of the car. The alert Marines snapped to attention. She entered the church. A few minutes later she was back. Another woman was with her. Also in black with an even bigger veil. Amarena smiled at the alert Marines still at attention. Both women got into the limousine that drove away rapidly towards the traffic circle. The courteous Marines noted that it was getting light in the east.

He woke up. He was stretched out on the cell floor. The stench. Why was the stench so strong? Handcuffed again. His clothes scattered everywhere. The stench, the stench? Cold. Cold, cold and pain. Pain. Stench. Screams in the distance. He could hear them. Pain. Stench. Pain, pain and cold. He was afraid to look, to see himself. Between his legs?

Now we're on the highway. Take off that ridiculous veil, cutie.

Where are we?

Near San Lucas.

Amarena.

Everything's arranged.

Voices in the corridor again. There were voices in the corridor. It was no dream. He recognized the voices. No. No, no. No. No more! Looked all around the cell. There was no place. No. No more! They opened the door. No! They laughed at him. No, no. Let's see if you talk now, you sonofabitch. No more, no. They laughed. They applauded. No more, no. Let's see if you talk now, you sonofabitch.

Kids, did you sleep well?

The woman standing in the doorway. She was very stout. And had a resonant voice.

Did you sleep well? I asked.

Pacha felt around for his eyeglasses. Rodri was already up, smiling.

Jeezus! Just fine. Thanks.

He had only his trousers on. She could see the ribs on his chest sticking out. The short little arms, all muscle.

One of the girls will bring your breakfast. It would be better if you didn't leave the room.

Yes, yes, of course.

The boys amused her. That shyness, that soft skin vibrant with energy. Always doing as they were told. She would have liked to go in and pet them, to see how their eyes tried to avoid hers. But she had to supervise the girls.

Ma'am. Thanks very much. Once again. For letting us spend the night.

No problem. She knew the Minister of Defense well. They would never dare touch her place. She smiled. She knew the Minister of Defense only too well. She closed her eyes to see that skinny young man again, tall, her only son, her only love, that young man with the thin mustache like silk stained with wine whom she hadn't seen since '54.

There it is.

The limousine parked beside the highway. She looked at the hunchbacked woman wrapped in mist. Pure rock. Thick pine woods on both sides. The Sierra Madre further behind, like Amarena's spine, mountain after mountain in the distance, rough country, undulating, a sea of curves, green curves, not a single straight line, the curves of the mountain tops, bright green, green that kills, as though seen through Pacha's fogged-up glasses.

There it is.

He got out of the limousine and began to run up. He could already smell the odor of incense and tallow. Incense and tallow. He ran up to the top without a stop.

There it is.

She walked behind him. She had heard the story on the way. He told it to her. About the old man. About Tecún Umán and the Quichés. About Princess Alxit. About dying first rather than surrendering to the foreign invader. There were a lot of brilliantly colored stones all around.

At the tip of the world, Amarena! What a place! The very spot where she stabbed herself, the very spot he made me promise to visit some day. He told me my first story. He told me about the power of the word. He told me about my father and the bombs. He told me I would be standing here one day...

You're scared brainless. Has the moon gotten to you?

Words are sacred, Amarena. "Spider" Arana! Country of green trees! And there you have it. It's a way of making all things yours. That's why when the Indians come here to pray, they say after lighting the candles: *The word, everything. Outside the word, nothing.* In the word, the world, Amarena. It's a way of making it yours.

And what would I do with it? Butter and salt it and eat it up?

He heard the door open. No... Ready... No... He wouldn't open his eyes... The laugh... for more? No... the music... Twist! Twist! Twist!... The laugh... They would go away if he didn't open his eyes... No. He felt a hand on his ankle. It was warm. The laugh... They were pulling him... No more... He was slipping. He was slipping into a dream... No... He was a child... The dogs were barking... The laugh... It was warm underneath. Cold on top. Ready for more? No. The dogs were barking. Alsita screamed... The music...

When Máximo woke up in the Union Church he did not recognize the gray walls. Did not remember the trip back. But then he saw her sitting on the edge of the bed, smiling. He caught a glimpse of the sunset through the little window.

I have to go now. But I'll be back in a couple of hours. I left my food on the table.

Where to? Where are you going?

To pick up your plane ticket.

My plane ticket?

Your plane ticket. In case you didn't know, brother, you have to catch the midnight flight...

Holy shit! That soon?

But first a little farewell party that's going to be sensational. You'll see. But right now I have to run.

She slammed the door behind her and he could hear her quick footsteps echoing through the courtyard. He began to bite his pacifier. He was leaving! This very night! How? He went for his jar of Vicks. He was leaving. Just like that. He stuffed his nostrils with Vicks. What about his mother? But what else could he do? What else? What to do, parrot! *All against the wall!* Prison, death or exile. Make a choice, then, nothing else to do. He turned to the copy of *Don Quixote* he had found, torn, dusty, gnawed by mice in a forgotten bookcase in the church. Reading the truth in words, a diplomatic perk.

> If Adelita went off with another
> I'd go after her by land or by sea
> If by sea in a warship,
> If by land in a military train.

The music had begun. The Flames specially hired for the great occasion. They were playing from the altar and began with their famous salad. The benches had been cleared. Everybody was dancing in the nave of the church. It was a masquerade ball, of course.

> Back on the farm
> when I was young and free

A little farm girl there would smile
and say to me

Rodri and Pacha were there. They had just
arrived after having spent the whole day with the
woman who knew the Minister of Defense only too
well. Rodri hopped first on one leg, twisting at the
waist from side to side, bending backwards, throwing
his arms in the air and yelling. Oh, Jeezus! He was
dressed as a medieval page all in gold, with red
stockings, and white makeup on his face. Oh, Jeezus!
And standing on the other leg, applauding, shouting
Twist! Twist! Twist!

I'll sew you a pair of trousers
Just like the farmers wear

Pacha was dancing without moving above the
waist, his knees pumping up and down, a smile
frozen on his face, applauding, one, two, three, his
huge sailor's costume flying all around him, one,
two, three, much too big for him, much.

I'll start them out with wool
And finish off with leather.

And the whores were there, twisting, twisting,
all dressed up as Carmelite nuns, holding up the
hems of their habits and kicking their legs up and
down, up and down in classical cancan style.
Dancing, dancing wildly to wipe away the present,
jumping up high, yelling, leaping, sweating, dancing
to wipe away the bad dreams of sad nights, holding
hands to face the future. The Flames up on the main

altar, five shirts of gold sequins and tight black pants, and loudspeakers in every corner of the church.

> If I die on your account
> Scorned by your cruel heart

And waiters in tuxedoes with white jackets running back and forth with trays of champagne glasses, perspiration streaming from their foreheads which they kept wiping with the palms of their hands. The people waylaid them, reaching under their arms, under their legs, from behind, bared arms grabbing for the golden liquid as if it were their last chance in life, pouring half the contents of the glasses over the unfortunate waiters who swore at them. Outside, the alert Marines had the church surrounded and would not allow in the police and soldiers who had been sent to check up on the ruckus, claiming that it was an exclusive affair of the American colony over which the natives had no jurisdiction, nor was it any of their *business*. They could not allow them in without a direct order from the ambassador whose phone didn't happen to answer that night.

> If your kisses make me die
> No prisoner happier than I.

All the soccer players were there, disguised as whores wearing see-through blouses with deep decolleté, short tight little skirts, and huge falsies. And Amarena in a white dress covered with veils, dancing in a circle. Turn after turn, the veils floating, hanging in the air, her long black hair floating in the

210

air, free. Both her lipstick, and her nails painted bright green with silver dots, and a Lone Ranger mask of the same colors over her eyes. She got up on her toes, raised one leg, her eyes closed, describing circles in the air with one arm, the other resting in Máximo's hand.

> I don't love you anymore, sausage nose
> Go home to mommy
> and have her fix it for you
> I don't love you anymore, turkey nose
> Go home to mommy
> and have her pull it off you.

He wearing a splendid U.S. Army uniform, an officer's dress uniform complete with necktie and highly polished shoes, he turning Amarena around and around, swinging her around him. Not a dark hair left on him, the dye job a triumph. He was as blond as Tonadiú, the new uniform a bit stiff, the shoulders rather tight, and the name plate on his breast said Lt. Shotwell, she twirling around him, turn after turn, the veils floating, suspended in the air, black hair floating in the air, free, the loyal parrot on his left shoulder and he executing turns, turns, turns and how soft her hands were.

> I won't be crying anymore.
> If she wants to go, let her go.
> I won't be crying anymore.
> If she wants to go, let her go.

And time moved on, second by second, minute by minute. He was leaving. And the crowd dancing,

dancing like exorcists, dancing wildly, turning and turning and twisting and leaping and whistling and sweating and yelling and weeping and guzzling and turns and turns and turns, embroidered silk vests, throaty voices, jealous males. Ha, ha, hayee!

The brothers Pinzón were all

Students and whores dancing, artists venturing out of the dusty holes in which they hide.

wild sailors.

Harlequins and clowns, Carmelite nuns and whores, tight sweaters, short coats, old trousers, sheer stockings. There was a man with a fur hat and a shepherd's crook. Another with a dirty canvas suit and a shirt made of paper with a necktie drawn on it in India ink.

And they went to the Azores
To check out the

Awful looking masks everywhere, and huge bellies.

...shores

There were dolls, puppets, toys, all jumping, the music getting louder all the time, loud, The Flames jumping up and down, up and down on the main altar, knocking the objects off the altar every which way. The crash of the falling pieces interfered with the sound, provoking whistling and protests, glasses and china flying across the room.

But the Indians climbed down the walls and kicked them in the

And the people ducking out of the way of the flying crockery and glassware. Amarena jumping and laughing and Máximo, the parrot beating its wings and screeching *All against the wall!* Máximo worrying about losing his army cap with the gilt eagle spreading its great wings.

...brawls.

Two men hanging from the chandeliers, kicking glasses and plates off trays.

And conked their brother Pinto

Her long black hair flying, and his olive-green uniform, spinning around and their arms together, linked, spinning around and their arms together,

with a bottle of vino tinto.

And then the clock struck the hour. Amarena stopped dancing. She stood in the middle of the nave, looking at it, at the clock. The music stopped. The dancers froze in place. They pulled a table covered with a burlap bag into the center of the room. All at once Rodri was on the table giving an impassioned speech peppered with jokes. The people applauded, the Carmelite nuns threw themselves on the boy to embrace him, flowers flew through the air, a couple of poets pushed Rodri off the table and began reciting poems that tried to rhyme. Everybody was astonished. Poems hadn't been heard in public since how long ago? Words came back to life. Speech! Speech! the crowd was shouting. They brushed Amarena aside and pushing Máximo onto the table, stood him up there, the applause continuing, the applauding, and the parrot *All against the wall!* applauding, and flowers raining down. Nervously downing the last drops of his drink.

Leave here and make the generals laugh. Kill them with laughter. Laugh and live. Let the vultures gorge themselves on despair. Remember. Words are life. The word is immortal, the word is invulnerable to bullets, the word may be dormant but will never die.

Music, shouts, flowers erupting once more, madness, orgiastic convergence, Máximo swept from the table onto the shoulders of the crowd carried the length of the nave, the last of the glasses breaking, tears streaming down, streamers and confetti flying, some of the whores starting to undress. The crowd broke through the doors of the church and burst out into the street in their disguises. The alert Marines were swept along by the torrent of human bodies, ending up in the fountain at España Square. The Flames, transported altar and all, on an open truck that headed the great parade. The music continued torturing the city.

The scorpion, pion-pion,
The scorpion, pion-pion

Gonna sting me.
Get your shotgun, grandma, and kill it
And if it don't go off,
Hit it with a skillet.

Several bands joined them in the street, marching and dancing behind the truck, people kissing, hugging, throwing confetti, and Máximo and Amarena holding hands lost in a liberating sea of noise. Sirens began to be heard but the people paid no attention. A bald-headed man drew his pistol and shot off the end of his nose.

I don't know, don't know, don't know
But it's a disgrace
It's a disgrace
What's happenin' to this place.

They marched down the Avenue of Supplications and passed along the Avenue of Freedom, by an obscure corner, up Montúfar Avenue, passed before the attentive eyes of the Chinese magician who was threading needles with his mouth while standing on one foot and twisting, twisting, twisting, the crowd, twisting, destroying the thorny plants that grew in the cracks of the pavement, twisting, twisting, twisting, knocking over the dead bushes and withered trees, twisting, twisting, twisting, sweeping pieces of glass and dead leaves from the street, crushing the little mounds of mouldering brick into powder. The pavement began to give.

Let's go down by the bull-bull-rushes

215

And see Doña Ana
feeding berries to the thrushes.

Máximo and Amarena holding hands, Máximo
and Amarena exchanging kisses, Máximo and
Amarena hip to hip, Máximo and Amarena,
Máximo and Amarena, twist twist twist, Máximo
and Amarena, Máximo twist twist twist and
Amarena. He trying to resist the urge to stop at The
Last Goodbye to have one for the road.

What did your lordship wish,
matadero tero la?
I wished for a baby girl,
matadero tero la.

Huge frightened rats ran by, escaping the
approaching throng, flowers against the starry sky,
the first shots. People falling, people dancing, twist
twist twist. Children sitting on the walls watching
the parade. The neighbor of a nervous oligarch
shooting at them, obliging them to get down off the
blood-covered walls.

There was a pretty fountain
That had a little jet
That grew tall and then very small
But always stayed wet.

Down the Avenue of Liberation, breaking the
pavement on the Avenue of Liberation, dancing
around the flying bullets, leaping, obliterating the
Avenue of Liberation, negating the Avenue of
Liberation, and Airport Avenue in sight. In sight.

Amarena turned to look at him, at Máximo, her nails digging into his hand. One of the whores tripped.

> Don't keep threatening and threatening me
> all day long
> You've made up your mind
> to start a new life
> So get to where you're going,
> get going, begone.

And down Airport Avenue. Both sides of the street lined with silent people. The entire way to the empty terminal hidden by cypresses. The silent people waving their handkerchiefs. The volcanoes in the distance. Máximo saw an empty can in the middle of the street. He kicked it hard trying to score in the mouth of the sewer. The can slid along the pavement straight into the black opening. Finally. Goal.

> If it's your fate to give me the gate
> You must know what you're doin'
> You say I'm on my way on my way,
> > on my way
> And still you don't get goin'.

And outside the terminal. Máximo jumped into a pickup truck. And Amarena. Pacha and Rodri. The Flames still going full blast. They could see the police coming down the avenue. The dogs howling with hunger, the neighbors waking up, the lights going on all over the city.

And I'm waiting for your love,
waiting for your love
Or waiting for you to forget me.

Oh Jeezus! We're going to make it! Put this top hat on. You can hide the parrot under it. If not, they won't let you take him on the plane. But with this thing, on, here it is just in case, what a fucked-world. They'll know you're coming from a party.

What about you?

We're leaving. Pacha and I. We're getting out of here. Now that you did your thing and fucked up our placid way of life we're going to the Petén. To look for the Mayan ruins we were telling you about.

It's a good time of year for the jungle, you know. The mosquitoes are on strike. Not much rain but enough water. We know a guide.

Máximo. Talking to the end. Get off the platform. Here. Your ticket. Passports. Health certificate. Everything in order.

A ticket for around the world! I can go anywhere. London, Paris, Rome, Beirut, Teheran, Bombay, Singapore. Unbelievable! And two passports. American and Swiss. Where did you get them?

A diplomatic secret. Now hurry. Get going.

Okay, Máximo. This is it, Jeezus. Our guide is waiting for us. Over there at the end of the runway. We've got to get out of here. But. We'll be seeing you. Jeezus. Remember to keep those legs in shape. Lots of soccer still to be played in this world. And don't go forgetting the mother tongue on us and come back talking through your nose.

What little confidence you have! It's in my mind and my heart, man.

Sure, till you shack up with your first little Dutch girl.

Pacha and Rodri jumped out of the pick-up and took off running for the darkest corner of the airfield. They turned and waved goodbye, turned and waved goodbye, turned until they were swallowed by the darkness. The pick-up stopped beside the wheels of the plane. Máximo and Amarena jumped down and started running under the huge wing.

Where did you get them?

From Mr. Wright.

Who's he?

A friend of my father's.

The police and soldiers arrived at the airport terminal. The whores still wearing their habits assembled at the main entrance and held up their rosaries. The soldiers and police knelt before them. The whores began reciting the words of *The CIA Man*. On the other side, The Flames brought their musical salad to its inevitable conclusion.

> This is the mambo, this is the mambo
> This is the heelbeat mambo.
> The heelbeat, the heelbeat
> The heelbeat mambo.
> Tiriboom tiriboom tiriboom poom poom!
> Tacatacatacatacatacataca boom!

All the lights in the city were on. The uproar could be heard throughout the city, throughout the city the uproar could be heard. The uproar could be heard at the Gardens of Utatlán and at La Florida.

The echoes reached clear to La Palmita and the residents of Vista Hermosa were surely hearing it. The uproar. It was heard in El Sauce and the residents of La Parroquia could hear it. It could be heard in the Centroamérica section and by the residents of Atlantida. It loosened the foundations of the Roosevelt Hospital. The uproar. It made the bell ring at the top of the Reforma Tower. The uproar. The pale green paint on the stadium flaked off. The wall on the right side of the Cathedral cracked. The Archbishop saw the crack and began to tremble hiding his face in the sexton's chest. The uproar. It shook the presidential residence and General "Spider" Arana ran out to the patio in his shorts. He tripped over the drain, began jumping up and down on one foot, fell back against the column, dislodging tiles on the ceiling of the corridor. The tiles came down in a cloud of red dust. Only his bare feet were sticking out from under the heap of tiles that piled up on top of him. He was still moving his big toes.

What about you, what are you going to do now?

Hurry, man! They've announced your flight. And keep that top hat on.

Won't you come later? Couldn't we meet somewhere?

I can't. I have to pay off Mr. Wright for those precious documents. Now, get going, man!

How much?

Idiot! It's with me I'm...

The stewardesses were pulling him by the sleeves, suspiciously eyeing the top hat. You're going to miss your flight, lieutenant, they said. Máximo reassured them, patting them on the back. He looked towards the main entrance. The soldiers were still kneeling before the pious nuns, listening solemnly to their litany. Amarena noticed that his pacifier was gone.

Where's your pacifier? Did you lose it?

He considerd the whores. He looked at Amarena. Will you take care of my mother? Yes. Will you tell her where I am, that everything's all right? Yes. Promise? Yes. He kissed her. You'll miss your flight, lieutenant. Máximo turned towards the plane. His face was completely clear, not a trace of his allergy to be seen. He bounded up the steps, singing the wonderful mix of songs that had come together to form a great salad. Amarena watched him as he went.

1973-1975

Related titles available from Curbstone

HAVE YOU SEEN A RED CURTAIN IN MY WEARY CHAMBER, selected writings by Tomás Borge; edited & trans. by Russell Bartley, Kent Johnson & Sylvia Yoneda. This first U.S. publication of Borge's poetry, essays and stories offers insight into this man, his work and the Nicaraguan Revolution. $9.95pa. 0-915306-81-6.

ASHES OF IZALCO, a novel by Claribel Alegría and Darwin J. Flakoll, trans. by Darwin J. Flakoll. A love story which unfolds during the bloody events of 1932, when 30,000 Indians and peasants were massacred in Izalco, El Salvador. $17.95cl. 0-915306-83-2; $9.95pa. 0-915306-84-0.

LUISA IN REALITYLAND, a prose/verse novel by Claribel Alegría; trans. by Darwin J. Flakoll. A retrospect of the real, surreal and magical memories of childhood in El Salvador into which the realities of war gradually intrude. $17.95 cl. 0-915306-70-0; $9.95 pa. 0-915306-69-7.

MIGUEL MARMOL, by Roque Dalton; trans. by Richard Schaaf. Long considered a classic testimony throughout Latin America, *Miguel Marmol* gives a detailed account of Salvadoran history while telling the interesting and sometimeshumorous story of one man's life. $19.95cl. 0-915306-68-9; $12.95pa. 0-915306-67-0.

GRANDDAUGHTERS OF CORN: Portraits of Guatemalan Women by Marilyn Anderson & Jonathan Garlock. These photographs of Guatemalan women are accompanied by text that provides background for understanding the cultural as well as political realities in this turbulent country. $35.00cl. 0-915306-64-6; $19.95pa. 0-915306-60-3.

TESTIMONY: Death of a Guatemalan Village by Victor Montejo; trans. by Victor Perera. *Testimony* gives an eyewitness account by a Mayan school teacher of an army attack on a Guatemalan village and its aftermath, told in a clean and direct prose style. $16.95cl. 0-915306-61-1; $8.95pa. 0-915306-65-4.

THE SHADOW BY THE DOOR by Gerardo di Masso; trans. by Richard Jacques. This novel takes place during the "dirty war" in Argentina and describes how a torture strives to maintain his sanity by recalling an adolescent love affair. $6.95pa. 0-915306-76-X.

FOR A COMPLETE CATALOG, SEND A REQUEST TO:
Curbstone Press, 321 Jackson St., Willimantic, CT 06226